Grandpa, Tell me More Stories

More Educational, Entertaining, Moral packed, Short Stories for Children.

Ideal Bedtime Stories

D1521266

Sahasranam Kalpathy

ACKNOWLEDGEMENTS

I wish to thank Dr Mohan Leslie Noone who despite being busy with his medical profession, administrative responsibilities, and Digital commitments, for having gracefully agreed to write the Foreword for this second book of stories.

My thanks are also due to Mr. Raman Namboothiri who has designed a beautiful front cover for this book with an apt image.

My thanks are due to the readers of the first book of stories for children and their enthusiastic reviews and feedback, for it was their encouragement and feedback that made this second book possible.

Foreword

The stories we share form a core part of our identity; we grow up listening to them. Stories inspire and teach us the ways of the world, and from time immemorial the master storyteller was a prized member of society. Great stories prepare us to deal with the challenges of life, their morals and lessons standing as lighthouses in our journey through the seas of life.

It is hence a matter of great delight to see that Dr Sahasranam, a senior cardiologist and hospital administrator, who is a teacher and mentor to me, has come out with a second volume of short stories. It is a matter of inspiration to see how he has taken up writing as he winds down his medical workload, which is a meaningful and valuable way to stay active. He always had an interest in story telling and it is evident that he has been collecting stories for a long time from various sources to form a rich inventory of ideas and themes to draw from.

The format is similar to the first book with each story being introduced with a short incident with his two grandchildren. This works very well to give a meaningful and exciting context with the reader being transported to a familiar and identifiable context. A feeling of joining in with the story telling process leads to a unique sense of engagement. The stories are suitable to be read out aloud or older children may choose to read themselves. Even for adults many of the stories are fresh takes on a wide variety of familiar themes, and I found myself enjoying reading them much more than I expected! I have no doubt these stories will warm your hearts, inspiring and teaching to live better lives, as all good stories should.

Dr Mohan Leslie Noone

Senior Consultant Neurologist

What made me write this book

The first book that I wrote named, "Tell Me a Story Grandpa", inspired me to write more books for children. There were enough moral packed stories that would qualify to be included in this book. So also, many of the stories taken from Indian Mythology also emphasized moral and ethical values. I felt that these should be shared with my young readers.

Reading as a habit was inculcated in me right from childhood when my parents used to insist that all of us read books and to that effect, we used to get subscriptions of children's magazines and books. The library in the schools and colleges that I studied also abounded in good books of all genres.

In addition, the teachers in my school, the St Joseph's Boys' High School in Calicut, where I studied up to the tenth grade always encouraged and motivated the students to read the old classics by Shakespeare, Dickens, Alexander Dumas, Conan Doyle, and others. Every student had to write a two-page precis of the books read every fortnight and submit it for scrutiny to the English teacher. As many of the teachers were Jesuit fathers, we had a very good training in school.

As I grew up, I wanted to write, but my professional commitments took out most of my time and the only outlet for my writing was in the college magazines during our school and college days. Unlike today, we had no other mode of entertainment other than the playing outdoor and indoor games, watching cinemas, and reading books and magazines.

I intended these stories to be read by the nine- to twelve-year-old kids. Also, they can be read to them with proper modulation and inflection as bedtime stories for them to grasp the meaning of morals and their importance. The stories are linked to everyday occurrences in the lives of my grandchildren so that they understand the practical application of the morals and values in day-to-day life. The reading habit is the greatest gift that a parent can give to his child.

In the stories there are references to epics like the Ramayana and Mahabharata. For further reading, the children must be encouraged to read these epics which are widely available in simple abridged form in many languages. These epics abound in stories which will be entertaining and educational to the kids.

I dedicate this book to my wife Mohana, who has stood by me like a rock through thick and thin and helped me write these stories, occasionally contributing stories which she has heard during the religious discourses. The stories are not entirely from my imagination. Many have been heard during religious discourses, seminars, read in various Tamil and Malayalam magazines and culled from various other sources.

For those of you who enjoy reading this book, I would like to add that the third series of stories for children predominantly based on Indian Mythology is also in its embryonic stage and will be out later as the third in the series

1st.December 2021   Sahasranam Kalpathy

(Dr.K.V. Sahasranam)

There are many little ways to enlarge your child's world. Love of books is the best of all. —Jacqueline Kennedy

Please provide your esteemed and honest feedback about the book through my email:
kvsauthor@gmail.com

URL: https://www.amazon.com/author/sahasranamkalpathy

Medium: https://medium.com/me/stories/public

Linked In: https://www.linkedin.com/in/sahasranam-dr-k-v-3231a13a/

Medium: https://medium.com/subscribe/@ramani2911

1. The Unlucky Fisherman

Jaya and Vijaya returned from school.

"Did you eat all the snacks that I gave you?", asked Amma from the kitchen.

"Yes, Amma", said Vijaya. "All the biscuits are over. Only the wrapper is there in my bag. I must trash it. I'll do it now."

Amma checked her bag and came up with the wrapper. There were three more biscuits in it. "How careless of you, Vijaya", Amma chided, "There were three biscuits in the wrapper, and you were going to throw it in the trash not caring to check it!"

Aha", I commented, "It is like the fisherman who got a bag of stones from the seashore and threw them into the sea thinking it was trash."

"Thathu, Thathu," the kids shouted. "Tell us that story".

And I told them the story of the Unlucky Fisherman…

. . . .

Once upon a time there lived a fisherman by the sea. Every morning he would go to sea in his small boat and catch fish for the day and come back in the evening. He would sell the fish in the nearby bazaar and use the money to buy food for his family. He was leading a hand-to-mouth existence.

The fisherman was always discontented and despondent. He used to pray to God to relieve him of this misery and make him rich. Every night he used to go to bed with a prayer. One night after his prayers he went to bed regretting his misfortune. At midnight, he heard a soft voice whispering in his ear. "Oh, fisherman, luck will favour you tomorrow. But you should know to recognise the opportunity when it comes, otherwise, you will lose the chance to be rich and happy. You will be given only one chance." The voice faded away. The fisherman suddenly woke up from his sleep. He did not know if this was a dream or whether an angel or fairy had spoken to him. He could not sleep that night thereafter.

The next morning, the fisherman got up early well before sunrise and went to the seashore. He was waiting for sunrise before launching his boat into the waters as still it was dark. He was hopeful that he would have a bounty catch that day. Having nothing else to do, he was ambling along the seashore. Suddenly his feet hit on something. He bent to pick it up and found that it was an old, dilapidated leather pouch. He proceeded to throw it into the sea when he noticed some jingling noise from within. Thinking that he had hit upon some treasure, may be of gold coins, he opened the leather pouch only to find some pebbles inside. He was utterly disappointed. He continued to walk along the seashore flinging one pebble after another into the sea cursing his luck as he went till the pouch was empty and only one pebble remained in his hand. As he raised his hand to throw the last pebble into the sea, the sun rose with all its brilliance in the eastern sky and the man found that the pebble in his hand glowed and sparkled in the orange rays of the rising sun.

The fisherman immediately brought the pebble close to his eyes to inspect it at close quarters, when to his utter dismay, found that what he was holding was not a worthless pebble, but a brilliant diamond. The fisherman to is utter chagrin realised that all the pebbles that he had thrown into the sea were real priceless diamonds. Fortunately, one diamond remained in his hand.

He regretted his impulsiveness in throwing the diamonds into the sea and felt sorry for having lost the golden opportunity to become rich. The voice on the previous day had warned him not to let the opportunity go, but he had been too hasty and careless and did not recognise it.

Moral: Recognise every opportunity and act on it. You never know what is hidden in 'trash'. Success will be yours if you make use of every opportunity.

2. The Charioteer

The whole family was seated around a table and my daughter was chopping carrots, Jaya and Vijaya were sitting on the floor playing 'Who do you want to be?'.

Jaya said, "I want to be a dresser and a beautician who can create different types of hair dos."

Vijaya retorted, "I will be a horse jockey."

Jaya burst out laughing, "Horse Jockey! Foolish! Who would want to be riding horses or driving horse drawn carriages? You must be mad".

This made Vijaya burst into an instantaneous wail.

Vijaya closed her ears with her palms.

It was up to me to pacify her, "Look here, Vijaya", I said above the rising wail, "Have you heard the story of the boy who wanted to become the driver of a horse driven cart.?"

Vijaya's wail was instantly cut off and both eagerly sat up, "Tell us that story, Grandpa" they said in unison.

I began telling the story of the Charioteer...

● ● ● ● ● ● ● ● ● ● ● ● ● ● ● ●

One day the teacher asked her students, "What do you want to become when you grow up." Many of the students came up with answers like doctor, engineer, lawyer, and teacher.

But one boy got up and said, "I want to drive a horse drawn carriage when I grow up." The whole class broke out laughing and the boy burst into tears.

The boy returned home sadly and broke down telling his mother what had happened in the class that day. The mother cheered him up and pointed to a picture on the wall. It was a picture of Lord Krishna sitting on a horse-drawn chariot with the reins of the horses in his hands expounding the *Bhagavad Gita* to Arjuna.

"You must become a charioteer like him", she said, "You should be known to the whole world as a very famous person".

Do you know who this boy was, he was Narendran who later grew up to be the famous Swami Vivekananda.

MORAL: Have a lofty goal in life.

Bhagavad Gita: A very important Hindu Scripture expounded by Lord Krishna during the battle of Mahabharata.

Lord Krishna: One of the Hindu Gods who incarnated as an ordinary person to destroy evil on earth.

3.   WHO IS A REAL DEVOTEE?

"Thathu", said Vijaya, "Jaya did not say her prayers after bathing today".

"She is lying", countered Jaya, "I said my prayers silently, that's why she did not hear me pray."

Both were complaining to me as I sat at my table typing a manuscript on my laptop. It was time for my Pomodoro break, and I said to them, "Ok, tell me have you heard the story of Narada who thought that he was the only real bhaktha compared to anyone else?"

"Oh Thathu," both children spoke in unison, "Tell us the story".

I began telling them the story of Who is a Real Devotee…

. . . .

One day Sage Narada met Lord Vishnu in Vaikunta.

"Come my dear Narada", said Lord Vishnu," What is the purpose of your visit?"

"I have a long-standing doubt, Oh Lord Vishnu", said Narada. "A lot of devotees pray to you daily, I wish to know who is the most favoured and the best *bhakta* of all", said Sage Narada.

"Why do you wish to know this", asked Lord Vishnu with a mischievous smile.

"Just curiosity, Oh Lord Vishnu", said the Sage.

"Ok, then go to the village in the South of *Bharath* called Vaikuntapuram and look for a person named Ponnan. He is my most esteemed and loved *bhaktha*. Observe him to learn about his bhakthi". Lord Vishnu said with a smile.

Sage Narada was stunned for a moment. He had considered himself to be the most loved *bhaktha* of Lord Vishnu as he was constantly chanting the Lord's name 'Narayana', 'Narayana'.

"Go to the village and stay close to Ponnan for one full day and then come back to me", said Lord Vishnu.

Sage Narada went the same night to Vaikuntapuram. He watched Ponnan from a short distance. Ponnan could not see Narada as the Sage was a *Deva* from heaven and hence invisible.

The next morning Ponnan got up early and had his bath. Before going to work in the fields, he chanted "Hari Om Narayana" once before he started work. He worked hard all day and at sunset came home and laid down his plough and had a bath followed by his frugal dinner. Before he retired to bed, he chanted "Hari Om Narayana" once more and went to sleep.

Sage Narada had been watching him all day from dawn to dusk and Ponnan was fully engaged doing a lot of chores the whole day silently and diligently.

Sage Narada felt annoyed, angry, and perplexed because Ponnan had chanted the Lord's name only twice during the whole day.

He returned to Vaikunta and accosted Lord Vishnu, "Oh, Lord, you told me that Ponnan was your most esteemed *Bhaktha*."

Smilingly, the Lord said," Yes, I said so. So, what?"

"Oh, my Lord", lamented the sage, "I chant your name Narayana thousands of times throughout the day, but Ponnan chants your name only once in the morning before going to work and once in the evening before retiring. How can he be a superior *Bhaktha*?"

"Narada", said the Lord, "Ponnan silently thinks of me and prays to me the whole day while doing his duties and his work. Okay, how many times did you think of me and chant my name today?"

Sage Narada was taken aback, "Oh Lord!", he said shamefaced, "Today, I was so engrossed in watching and observing Ponnan, that I did not think of you or chant your name at all," agreed Narada truthfully.

"See Narada", said the Lord, "You forgot to think of me while doing a single and simple job of observing Ponnan, whereas Ponnan remembers me twice daily even during his busy daily activities and all day long. Now, you tell me who is a real *Bhaktha*?".

Narada hung his head in shame and humility.

MORAL: Never overestimate your capabilities or underestimate those of others.

Bhaktha: Devotee

Bhakthi: Devotion

Narada: An itinerant Sage from Hindu Mythology

Vishnu: One of the Trinity in Hindu Mythology.

Vaikunta: The Abode of Lord Vishnu.

Deva: A celestial god

Pomodoro break: A break taken frequently while doing some tasks. (About once in 25 minutes)

4   The Three Boons

"Thathu, Thathu," cried Vijaya, I got only nine almonds, Jaya has ten."

"I cannot give Vijaya one from mine", said Jaya, "Because then she will have ten and I will have only nine. It is unfair." This quarrel went on till my elder daughter gave one more almond to Vijaya and evened the score.

"You are arguing like silly children", I said, "You should learn to be contented with what is given to you and not hanker for more. Be satisfied with what you get, or else, you will end up like the man who was not contented even with the three boons that he got from God."

"Oh, Thathu," both of then squealed with delight, tell us that story.

And I began telling the story of the Three Boons…

. . . .

Once a man prayed intensely to God and wanted boons from Him. God was so moved by his devotion that he appeared before the man and said, "My son, I am pleased with your prayers. You may wish for any three boons, which I will grant you".

The man thought for a moment and said, "Oh, Lord! I will ask for one boon now and the other two later."

"So be it," said God, "Whatever you wish in your mind will come true".

The man had been nagged by his wife all these years for not having earned enough, and being lazy; hence on the spur of the moment, he wished that his wife was dead.

"He said," Oh! Lord, kindly relieve me from my wife's tyranny and I wish she were dead!"

His wish came true immediately and his wife died.

All his friends and relatives came to visit him and every one of them was praising the various good qualities that his wife had. "Oh! You had such a wonderful wife who had so many virtues," they said, "She was a generous soul always willing to help the poor and the needy. You are indeed very unlucky to have lost such a lovable and noble wife".

The man now realised that despite her shortcomings, his wife had so many virtuous qualities. He regretted his initial hasty wish and prayed again to God before the funeral ceremonies were over.

"Oh God," he pleaded, "Kindly return my wife alive to me so that I can live happily with her."

"So be it," said God.

Thus, his second boon was granted, and his wife was got up from the bier as if rising from her sleep.

Months rolled by.

A third boon remained to be asked and the man was very confused as to what to ask for. He could ask for wealth, power, kingdom, good children, excellent health etc., but he was not sure what to ask for. Finally, one day he prayed to God earnestly and God appeared before him in all splendour.

"Oh, God, I am confused as to what to ask for as my third and last boon – I am not sure what to ask for. Please guide me as to what is the best boon I should ask for."

God smiled, "My dear son, the greatest boon anyone can ask for is 'contentment'. Be content with what you have. Do not be greedy for the wealth of others, for kingdoms or for gold. Be good, do good. In life you will always get what you deserve, not what you covet. If you learn to be content with what you get in life you will be the happiest person on earth"

The man then asked for 'Contentment' and God said, "So be it".

The devotee and his wife lived a happy contented life ever after and God blessed them with many intelligent and devoted children and enough wealth.

Moral: Be content with what you have. You will always get what you deserve, not what you covet.

5. Pride and Charity

Jaya and Vijaya came bounding from school one evening. Thathu, Jaya was bubbling with energy." I did a great charity donation today."

"What did you donate, dear?", I asked.

"I got ten dollars as my pocket money for Vishu and I donated five dollars to a fund for orphans to buy books!", Jaya was beside herself with pride.

"Well done, good job", I congratulated her. But don't be carried away with these small acts of charity, for it may not be enough to fetch you Brownie points in heaven. Just like what happened to Yudhishtra when he was taken to Suthala to visit the banished king Mahabali."

"Thathu, squealed both girls in delight, we want to know that story"

Then I began telling the story of Yudhishtra's Pride and Charity…

. . . .

After the Mahabharatha war was over, King Yudhishtra was ruling his kingdom from Hastinapura. He was very charitable and philanthropic. Slowly, Yudhishtra came to overestimate himself and an iota of pride and arrogance about his philanthropy crept into his mind.

Lord Krishna noticed this and wanted to teach Yudhishtra a lesson in humility and curtail his pride.

Lord Krishna invited Yudhishtra to accompany him to *Suthala* (Netherworld). The King Mahabali (who had been exiled to *Suthala* by Lord Vishnu in his Vamana *Avathara*) was ruling the nether world, *Suthala*.

Lord Krishna and Yudhishtra on reaching *Suthala* were very hungry. They were given various types of food, fruits and items served in golden plates upon the order of King Mahabali.

After having enjoyed a sumptuous meal, Lord Krishna and Yudhishtra returned the empty plates to the servants. But the servants refused to accept the plates.

Both were surprised at this. The servants said," Here in *Suthala*, in our King Mahabali's rule, we never take back anything that we give including the plates. Lord Krishna with a mischievous smile looked at Yudhishtra and said, "In King Yudhishtra's kingdom, about five hundred hungry and poor people are given free food (*Annadanam*) every day.

"Oh", said the servants, "In that case we assume that there are at least five hundred people in Yudhishtra's regime who are poor and not able to get their daily food! We are sorry to hear that. But here, in *Suthala* we have no one who will accept free food as no one is 'poor'," said the servants of Mahabali.

Yudhishtra felt ashamed and humiliated. His pride was completely shattered now. He hung his head in shame.

Moral: Never be proud of what you are or what you do. Never underestimate others.

Vishu: A festival in India occurring in the middle of April when elders give gifts and money to the young and children.

Yudhishtra: The eldest of the Pandavas in the epic *Mahabharatha*

Suthala: One of the netherworlds which is akin to heaven

Mahabali: A great king in Hindu Mythology who was generous and benevolent but was banished to Suthala because he became arrogant.

Mahabharatha War: A great war fought between the Pandavas and Kauravas as described in the epic *Mahabharatha*.

Hasthinapura: The capital of the kingdom ruled by Yudhishtra

Avathara: Incarnation (of Lord Vishnu)

6   Bhima and Karna

Vijaya was happy today. She came bounding down the stairs after changing into casuals on returning from school. "Thathu", she said, "I did something great today. Ask me what?"

"What great task did you do today?", I asked with a sly smile.

"I gave one candy each to my three friends. Amma had given me ten candies when I went to school in the morning".

"That is commendable", I complimented her with a tap on her cheek, "Keep up the good work, but do you know what Bhima and Karna did when Krishna asked them to donate gold coins?", I asked, knowing fully well that it was time for my next story.

"Thathu, tell us that story now itself shouted both together", and I began telling the story of Bhima and Karna…

. . . .

Everyone praised Karna as a very philanthropic and charitable king. He used to donate whatever anyone asked him without thinking twice. His altruistic nature was famous far and wide and often was the envy of other kings too.

Once, Bhima accosted Lord Krishna, "Why everyone praises Karna for his generosity and charity. What is so great about him?" Bhima's words carried a tinge of jealousy.

Lord Krishna smiled mischievously. He wanted to teach Bhima a lesson. He said, "Okay, I will show you why Karna is praised by all. Meet me tomorrow at dawn."

There were large bundles of hay lying in the field, left there by farmers after the harvest. Lord Krishna converted one such large bundle into gold coins and turned to Bhima. "Bhima, you should donate all this gold before sunset today."

Bhima became enthused. He summoned all the poor and the weak in the village and adjoining villages before noon and started donating a basket full of gold coins to each of them. He continued to do so, as the day waned. By sunset he had donated only three-fourths of the gold. The sun went down and there was a huge pile of gold left. Bhima could not face Lord Krishna as he could not complete the task by sunset.

Lord Krishna smiled and called Karna the next morning and showed him another similar pile of gold coins. He said, "Karna, I want you to donate this pile of gold before sunset".

Karna agreed and went back to his palace. By noon, Karna came to Lord Krishna's palace and said that he had already donated all the gold. Bhima, hearing this, was surprised. Lord Krishna smiled enigmatically.

Lord Krishna and Bhima accompanied Karna to the place where the gold had been. There was no gold there. "What happened to all the gold?" asked Lord Krishna, "What did you do with it?"

"Soon after you left the place where the gold was, a poor, emaciated Brahmin came to me asking for alms. I donated the whole gold to him".

Lord Krishna looked at Bhima with a triumphant smile. Bhima hung his head in all humility accepting defeat.

Moral: Give credit where it is due. Don't be envious of another person's good reputation. Don't be parsimonious when you donate.

Bhima: The second of the Pandavas as in the epic Mahabharatha

Karna: A king, really the eldest son of Kunti, mother of the Pandavas, born before she was married and who was abandoned as a child and brought up by a charioteer.

7. Bhishma's Test

"Thathu, I am not able to thread the needle with this thread," lamented Jaya one Sunday morning squinting at the needle in her hand. She was trying to thread a needle with a piece of thread whose end was frayed. It kept missing the eye of the needle.

"Look here, Jaya, you must first make the end of the thread pointed like this. Do it by wetting your finger and thumb like this", I demonstrated how to make the end of the thread pointed and then threaded the needle quickly. "You must use common sense like what the Pandavas did when Bhishma gave them a test."

Looking at their eager faces, I knew what the next comment would be. "Okay, okay," I said and told them the story of Bhishma's Test…

. . . .

The Pandavas and Kauravas were cousins. They were trained in archery, political science, and various arts by Bhishma. "You must be humble and at the same time courageous," Bhishma used to advise them. As their period of education was coming to an end, Bhishma called the Pandavas and Kauravas aside and said, "I will now give each group a test to see which group will intelligently pass the test."

Bhishma took them to a building and said, "Look here, there are two identical empty rooms in that building. You should completely fill those rooms with whatever you consider appropriate so that every nook and corner of the room is filled and not an inch of space is empty and not filled. You may choose whatever you like to fill them with." Being the eldest of the two clans, Bhishma gave one key each to Duryodhana and Yudhishtra.

Duryodhana smiled sarcastically, "Oh! Such a simple task", he sneered, "I thought that the test would be a difficult one". He called all his ninety-nine brothers and pointed to a very large stack of hay lying in the courtyard of the palace. He told them to fill the room with enough hay so as not to leave even an inch of space.

The Pandavas, on the other hand fell into deep thought, "What shall we do?", said Bhima, the second brother of the Pandavas. If Bhishma *acharya* gives us such a task which looks simple prima facie, then there must be some catch in it", said Arjuna, the third of the Pandavas.

The brothers looked at Yudhishtra hoping that he would say something. The words of Bhishma, 'using your intelligence' was ringing in his ears. He smiled and said, "Don't worry, we will do it tomorrow morning".

The next morning Bhishma came to the building to inspect the results. Firstly, he opened the room given to Kauravas. He saw the hay and grimaced. On pressing with his hand, Bhishma created a large hole in the hay and told Duryodhana, "See there is a hole here which you did not fill". Duryodhana was at a loss to reply.

Next, he came to the room given to the Pandavas. When he opened the room, he was greeted with a sweet fragrance. At the centre of the room stood a lamp with five wicks. It was glowing, filling the room with light. A pan of incense stood nearby.

The room was filled with bright light from the lamp and sweet fragrance from the incense. "We filled the room with light and fragrance," said Yudhishtra.

Bhishma was immensely pleased, "You have rightly and intelligently passed the test", he said, "I am pleased with all five of you". Seeing this Duryodhana and his brothers fumed with jealousy and envy, but they had to accept defeat reluctantly, though.

Moral: Solving many problems requires intelligence and common sense rather than strength and power.

Pandavas: The five brothers in the Mahabharatha epic, cousins to the Kauravas

Kauravas: The hundred brothers in the Mahabharatha epic, cousins of the Pandavas

Bhishma: The grand sire of the Pandavas and Kauravas

Acharya: Teacher, Guru

Yudhishtra: The eldest of the Pandavas

Duryodhana: The eldest of the Kauravas

8   Ravana's Advice

"We have holidays for the next whole week. It is the fall holidays!", declared Jaya and Vijaya flinging their satchels on the sofa as soon as they returned from school.

"But didn't your class teacher give you any homework to be done during the holidays?", Amma asked as she emerged from the kitchen carrying two glasses of milk for the kids.

"Yes, lots and lots", replied Jaya, "But I won't do the homework till the last day of the holidays".

"That is not correct", I interjected, "All good things must be done promptly and in time. Do you know what Ravana said about postponing good deeds?"

"Thathu" shouted the kids, "Tell us that Ravana story, we have nothing to do now as the holidays have started. You must tell us lots and lots of stories during these holidays."

And I began telling the story of Ravana's advice...

. . . .

The Rama-Ravana war was coming to an end. Ravana had been felled by Rama's arrows and was lying in the battlefield waiting for death to liberate him.

Rama called his younger brother Lakshmana and said, "Ravana is a man who has learned all the Vedas and Shastras. He is an adept in political science and is an ardent devotee of Lord Siva".

"Yes, brother, I have heard this about him", said Lakshmana, "But what has it to do with me?"

"Go to Ravana who is lying in the battlefield", said Rama, "Go to him and listen to what advice he has to give. Tell him that I sent you to him. He will understand why."

The ever-obedient Lakshmana went to the place where Ravana lay on the battlefield, his body studded with Rama's arrows. He was in agony.

"Come Lakshmana", Ravana accosted him, "You are the glorious brother of the mighty and honourable Rama. Tell me what I can do for you?"

Lakshmana, with folded hands said, "Oh! Lankeshwara (King of Lanka) my brother Rama has sent me to gain some pearls of wisdom and advice from you. Please enlighten me."

"Listen Lakshmana, "began Ravana, "Once upon a time I was mighty powerful. The *Navagrahas*, *Yama* and *Indra* bowed unto me. So, I wanted all the subjects in my kingdom to go to heaven. I wanted to abolish hell totally".

"To achieve this," continued Ravana, "I decided to construct a flight of stairs from my kingdom across the skies to reach heaven, so that my people could ascend to heaven unimpeded. I decided to appoint Yama to supervise this mega project. I decided to start work the next day."

"It was at this juncture that *Soorpanaka* barged into my court and interrupted me to talk about Rama, Sita and you. So, I postponed the decision of constructing the stairs from earth to heaven."

"Lakshmana," continued Ravana, "All of you know what happened after that. Look here Lakshmana, I postponed doing a good deed and I am suffering the consequences today. Hence, Lakshmana, whenever you think of doing something good, do it immediately or at the earliest. Don't postpone it (**Subhasya Sheegraa**)- *Good things must be done early*. This is my parting advice to you"

"Yes, mighty Lankeshwara," said Lakshmana bowing with all humility, "I will definitely follow your advice".

The King of Lanka, Ravana breathed his last, his mind cleared of the arrogance and haughtiness that had led to his defeat.

Moral: Even the proud and the haughty have something to teach us.

Rama: The Prince of Ayodhya who was exiled to the forest for 14 years as per the epic *Ramayana*

Ravana: The Asura (demon) king of Sri Lanka who abducted Rama's wife Sita.

Vedas: The earliest body of Indian Scriptures

Shastras: Precepts, Rules or a Book or Treatise of specialised Knowledge (Sanskrit)

Navagrahas: The nine planets represented as nine gods

Yama: The God of Death.

Indra: The God of the Devas or celestial beings

Soorpanaka: Ravana's sister who tries to seduce Rama and Lakshmana in the epic *Ramayana*

9. Lifespan

Vijaya was always hungry. Whatever she ate, she always wanted more. One day while eating cakes after dinner, Jaya said, "Amma, I want only one small piece of cake. My tummy is not all that good today. A small piece is enough for me."

Immediately, Vijaya intercepted, "Amma, give me that piece which Jaya does not want."

Being diabetic, I too opted for only a small piece of cake.

Immediately, Vijaya spoke up. "Give me Thathu's share also."

I laughed aloud when I heard this. "Do you know what happened when man asked Brahma to extend his lifespan to seventy years?"

Immediately, both girls piped up, "Thathu tell us that story."

And I ended up telling the story about man's Lifespan…

. . . .

Lord Brahma was engrossed in creation. First, he created the donkey and gave it a lifespan of sixty years. "Oh Brahma, sixty years is too much for me. Give me only thirty years, that's enough for me", pleaded the donkey.

"So it shall be," said Brahma and took away thirty years from the donkey's lifespan.

Next Lord Brahma created a dog and gave it a lifespan of fifty years.

The dog whined, "Thirty years is enough for me. Reduce my lifespan."

Brahma took away twenty years from the dog's lifespan.

Next, he created a monkey and assigned it a span of fifty years.

The monkey exclaimed, "My goodness, Oh, Lord Brahma, I cannot live for fifty years on this earth. Thirty years will do for me".

The Creator complied with the monkey's request and removed twenty years from the monkey's life also.

Since all the animals asked for a reduction in lifespan, Lord Brahma thought that man also would ask for a lower lifespan and gave him a lifespan of twenty years only.

Man was very upset, "Oh Lord Brahma, you are very unjust to me. I am the highest of all evolved species, and you gave me a lifespan of only twenty years on earth. You gave the donkey, dog, and the monkey more years of life than me. This is gross injustice", pleaded the man.

"What do you want then," asked Brahma,

"Give me all those extra years which you removed from the lifespan of the other three", said man.

"Are you sure, think again. Do you want those years I removed from the donkey, the dog and the monkey?", asked Brahma smiling mischievously. The man adamantly stuck to his demand.

"Alright, so it shall be", said Lord Brahma and granted man thirty years from the donkey, twenty years from the dog and twenty years from the monkey.

Thus, man lives the life of a human for the first twenty years of his life. The next thirty years, he slogs like a donkey carrying the burden of his family on his shoulders.

Then for the next twenty years, he keeps watch over his earnings and belongings like a watchdog.

The last twenty years he spends jumping around from place to place depending on his children to look after him and behaving like a restless monkey.

Thus, the years of man, borrowed from the donkey, the dog and the monkey are spent.

After all these creations, Bhagavan Brahma wanted to create a woman.

Well, he is still contemplating what lifespan to give her.

Moral: Be careful what wish to ask for. Because it may come true.

10 Who is the Evilest Person?

Vijaya came complaining to me one day after school. "Thathu, she said, "Jaya says that our neighbour Amit is a good boy, but I have always found him to be a bully and a bad guy. To Jaya, everyone is good. No one is bad."

"Look here, Vijaya", I commented there is no one who is good or bad. It is our view of people that makes us think so. Do you know what Sri Krishna told Duryodhana and Yudhishtra to do when such a controversy arose?"

"Thathu, shouted both, tell us that story now".

And I began telling them how Sri Krishna made Yudhishtra go and look for the Evilest Person…

· · · · · · · · · · · ·

Once Lord Krishna was walking in the palace gardens of Hasthinapura. Duryodhana, the cousin of Yudhishtra came to see him. While discussing many matters, Duryodhana suddenly asked him, "Krishna, why do you always say that Yudhishtra is straight forward, honest, sincere and truthful? And you always are criticising me saying that I am dishonest insincere and deceitful. Why is this so?"

Lord Krishna smiled and said, "Okay, Duryodhana, I will give you a simple test. Go to the village that you see beyond that river. Meet all the villagers there and come back to me after two days and tell me how many good, sincere, and honest people there are in that village."

"Sure," said Duryodhana. He crossed the river and set forth into the village.

Two days later, Duryodhana met Lord Krishna in the garden.

"Duryodhana," Lord Krishna addressed him, "What did you find in the village beyond the river?"

"Oh, Krishna," lamented Duryodhana, "I went into the village and met every villager there, and to my surprise there was not even one good person in that village. All the villagers were evil and dishonest. They speak only lies and deceive others when they get the chance."

Lord Krishna saw Yudhishtra standing a few paces away in the same garden. Lord Krishna beckoned to him and said, "Yudhishtra, I want you to go to the village that you see beyond that river and come and tell me how many of the villagers are evil, dishonest and liars."

"Definitely, Krishna," replied Yudhishtra, "I'll be back in two days and report to you." Saying so, Yudhishtra went across the river and reached the village.

Two days passed. Lord Krishna and Duryodhana were sitting in the garden seat talking matters regarding the state, when Yudhishtra joined them. "What happened, Yudhishtra," asked Lord Krishna smiling.

"My friend," replied Yudhishtra, "When I met all the villagers there, I found not a single person who was a liar, dishonest or evil. All of them are extremely good people."

Lord Krishna turned to Duryodhana with a cunning smile, "See, Duryodhana, you did not find a single good person there. All were evil. But Yudhishtra could not find a single evil person. All were good."

Lord Krishna continued addressing them. "When Duryodhana met the people, he was focussing only on evil and so everyone looked evil to him, whereas when Yudhishtra met them, he saw only the goodness in the villagers and never saw an evil person. It is because of your basic nature that you see goodness or evil in a person."

Duryodhana hung his head in shame.

Moral: You see the good in people if you are good and evil if you are not good. What you see in others is often a reflection of your own character.

Duryodhana: The Kaurava prince of Hastinapura who was the eldest of the one hundred sons of Dhritarashtra, the King.

Yudhishtra: The prince of Hastinapura who was dethroned by Duryodhana and exiled to the forest when he lost his kingdom to Duryodhana in a game of dice. (See the epic "*Mahabharata*")

11. Destiny

One day, Jaya came from school with a sad face. Throwing her satchel on the sofa, she sat and sobbed. "What happened?", I asked her concerned that she might have injured herself.

"Our maths miss Elsa had an accident today. While coming to school, the car she was driving hit against a tree on the side of the road because her brakes failed. Miss is in hospital.", she continued to sob.

Cheer up, Jaya", I said, "You cannot escape destiny. That accident happened because it was her destiny. Let us be happy that her injuries are only minor, and she will be home soon".

What is destiny?", asked both together. Tell us about it. And I began telling a story about Destiny…

■ ■ ■ ■ ■ ■ ■ ■ ■ ■ ■ ■ ■

Destiny is something that cannot be changed. It is something that is bound to happen or has happened to a particular person or thing; What happens in your life is called destiny. It is also called Fate. The story of the little sparrow elaborates it.

Once Yama, the King of Death visited *Vaikunta*, the abode of Lord Vishnu for a friendly chat. Even in those days, the guards at the entrance of Vaikunta, had to get permission from the Lord to allow anyone to enter. Hence, Yama had to wait outside in the garden for a few minutes till the guards returned.

As Yama was waiting, he glanced up at a nearby cherry tree and saw a tiny sparrow sitting there pecking at the cherries, chirping away happily. Yama fell deep into thought; something disturbed his mind.

Garuda, the eagle who was the vehicle for Lord Vishnu was sitting in a corner of the garden half asleep with one eye open, mindful of what was happening all around. He saw Yama watch the tiny sparrow thoughtfully, with his hand on his chin as if he was in deep thought. *Garuda* wondered, "What is Yama thinking about watching that bird?"

Soon the guards returned and bowed to Yama and accosted him inside.

Garuda thought, "Yama is the God of Death. If his sight falls on someone, it is an ill-omen. Death could befall that person. This poor little sparrow may be in for trouble. I must save it."

Thinking thus, Garuda came down from his perch and picked up the sparrow gently by his claws without hurting it and carried it far away from the eyes of Yama. Garuda flew over hills and dales and crossed the seven seas to a forest called *Dandakaranya*. He safely deposited the sparrow on the top of a rock there and returned to the garden in Vaikunta to his previous perch.

Yama, having finished his interlude with Lord Vishnu, came out of *Vaikunta* and once again glanced at the cherry tree where he had seen the little sparrow. When he saw that the sparrow was no longer there, his forehead creased into a questioning frown. He shook his head sadly and prepared to exit the garden when *Garuda* accosted him.

"Oh, mighty God of death, I observed you when you came and entered Vaikunta. Why did you look at that small sparrow thoughtfully when you entered? I thought that you had something in mind".

"Garuda" Yama addressed him condescendingly, "I know the future of all living beings thoroughly. I also know that no one can beat destiny. That little bird had only another half an hour to live when I saw it on the tree. But it was supposed to be devoured by a large snake in the Dandakaranya which is so far away, beyond the seven seas. I was wondering how this little bird with its tiny wings could cross the seven seas and reach Dandakaranya in such a short period of half an hour. It is already half an hour now and the bird should have been devoured now by the snake and its life ended".

Saying that, Yama left the garden.

Garuda stood shocked! Only then did he realize that he was also a part of destiny in causing the death of the little bird.

So, kids, destiny catches up whatever be our excuses. So always work hard with a positive mental attitude.

Moral: We must do our duty constantly and leave destiny to itself without worrying too much about it or trying to change it.

Yama: The God of Death in Hindu Mythology

Vaikunta: The abode of Lord Vishnu, one of the Hindu Trinity.

Garuda: A large eagle, said to be the vehicle of Lord Vishnu.

Dandakaranya: A dense forest in South India referred to in the epic *Ramayana*.

12. The General and the Soldier

My son in law had taken the kids, for their swimming lessons in the morning. It was a pleasant Saturday morning in the month of October. Every Saturday, they would go for their weekly swimming lessons.

When they came back, Vijaya was having a grouchy expression on her face.

"What happened/", I asked her, "Did your classes not go as usual?"

"It did Thathu", she said, "But Appa did not allow me to talk to my miss who was sitting on the opposite side of the swimming pool. I wanted to greet her and say, 'good morning' to her."

"Ha, ha", I laughed, "Is that the cause for this sour face? You should know when and where to greet a person. Don't be foolish like the soldier who saluted the general and made a mess of what he was doing".

That triggered off a spate of requests to me to tell the story and I began the story of the General and the Soldier…

············

Once a General and a soldier, who was his attendant were walking along a village. It was quite hot and there was no one visible anywhere nearby. The General was thirsty, and they were in search of water to drink. The soldier said that he would try to get some water from the nearby village.

The General went alone along the deserted village path. Suddenly he found a well near a thatched shed, but there was no one around. He bent down and peeped into the well to see if there was any water, but accidentally, his leg slipped, and he fell into the well with a huge splash.

The soldier who was going in search of help heard the splash and came back running and found that the General had fallen into the well.

"Oh, General Sahib, what a misfortune. How did you fall into the well?" Saying so, the soldier started weeping, for he was much attached to his master.

"Don't stand there staring and crying," the General shouted, "Go and fetch someone to help or try and find a rope and throw it to me".

The soldier saw that no one was around to help and ran to the shed nearby. In the shed, he was lucky to find a long thick rope and came running to the well with it. He could not find any tree nearby to tie the end of the rope. So being healthy and strong, the soldier held tightly to one end of the rope and dropped the other end into the well to help pull out the General. The General was pleased.

He held on to the rope and started climbing slowly getting a foothold on the wall of the well. The soldier being strong held on tightly to the rope and pulled the General up slowly.

At last, the General was almost at the end of his arduous climb and his head appeared above the edge of the well. The soldier having been trained to salute the senior members whenever they are seen immediately let go of the rope and stood to attention and gave the General a stiff and respectful salute!

Moral: Respect is to be given at the proper time and proper place.

13. The King's Astrologers

The Autumn holidays or the fall holidays, as the Americans say was starting the next week. My son in law and daughter had planned to take the kids on an outing to the nearby state to see the fall colours.

As soon as this was told to the children, Vijaya spoke up, "I don't want to go".

"But dear what happened?", asked Amma concerned.

"No, I don't want to go outing", Vijaya was adamant.

"Tell me why you don't want to go, dear", I asked employing a different tactic. "You must tell Thathu why you refuse to go".

"My maths miss has given us a lot of problems to solve and if I go with you, I will not be able to finish the homework before the school re-opens after the holidays. That is why I don't want to go", Vijaya's explanation made us all burst out laughing.

"Oh, dear", I decided to be tactful. "Your problem is simple. We can easily solve it by coming back one day earlier than planned. That will give us one extra day for you to solve your maths problems. I will also help you do your homework. I will talk to Appa".

Vijaya's face brightened, and she nodded smiling.

"Children", I said, "there are different ways of saying the same thing. Just like what two astrologers told the king."

"Oh Thathu", pleaded the kids, "the story please".

And I began telling them the story of the King's Astrologers…

· · · · · · · · · · ·

Once upon a time in a kingdom, there was a king who ruled his subjects with benevolence and strict discipline. But he had a violent temper. The king would punish any one on the spur of the moment if he said anything which brought him displeasure or dissatisfaction. Hence, most of the subjects, though they liked him, feared him, and hardly said anything to offend the king.

The king was getting old and was fifty-nine years old. He had planned to celebrate his sixtieth birthday with pomp and splendour being his *Shashtiabdapoorthi.* The plans for the grand function had already started and all the ministers were busy with the invitations and the arrangements for the celebrations. The king had invited many artists, pundits, performers, and astrologers from far and wide.

One day an astrologer walked into the king's court and greeted the king, "Oh Maharaj, he said, "I come from a faraway land and am the Chief astrologer of the king in that country. I have the knowledge to foretell the future with accuracy and the king there has decorated me with many awards."

The king greeted the astrologer and offered him a seat and said, "Oh, *pundit,* since you are a learned person, I want you to check my horoscope and tell me what the stars foretell about my future."

"Sure, Maharaj," the astrologer replied, I will calculate the position of your stars and let you know your future accurately. But today is not an auspicious day for checking horoscopes and as the sun will set soon, we can do it tomorrow, which is a very auspicious day."

The king was overjoyed, "Sure, oh pundit, you must be tired after your long travel. Go and rest in my guest house and come to the court tomorrow after a good night's sleep."

The pundit retired to his guest house and the next day after his daily rituals of prayers and *poojas,* came to the court of the king. The king was already in the court along with his courtiers, the queen, and his family. All were eager to hear what the astrologer had to say.

The astrologer seated himself on a small stool in front of the throne and opened the horoscope which was brought to him in a golden box. He took out the horoscope which was wrapped in red silk and put it on the small stand that was kept in front of him. The astrologer brought out a small pouch from his bag and took out a few white pearly seashells from them and after holding them in his hand and praying aloud for about ten minutes, scattered the shells on the floor in front of him. The astrologer, counted the shells that were on their belly and those that had fallen properly, made some calculations in his mind and then with a deep sigh looked up at the king and queen who sat in state in front of him in their thrones.

"Oh, Maharaja, he said with a crestfallen look, "You are very unlucky. A great misfortune is to befall you soon. Your wife and sons will be killed in an ambush by the king of a nearby kingdom and you will be left alone. This will happen after your sixty first birthday. It is very unfortunate, but it is the truth. The stars never lie".

Hearing this, the king was shocked at first. The shock gave way to rage. "How dare you tell me about such a bad omen?", the king thundered. Your predictions are all wrong and you will be imprisoned for your impertinence." Saying so, the king ordered his guards to put the astrologer in the dungeon and lock him up.

All the courtiers were worried that the king would lose his family after one or two years. A pall of gloom hung over the whole court.

Just then, another man in a silk turban came forward. "Honourable, Maharajah", he addressed the king, "I am an astrologer from a nearby kingdom and would like to take a second look at your horoscope and make predictions for the future."

"Very well," the king said, "I will give you a chance to find the truth behind this and I warn you that if your prediction is also similar, you will be punished. But you must tell the truth as it is."

The second astrologer, bowed before the king and said, "Maharajah, let me appease the Gods with a *Pooja* this evening and tomorrow I will study your horoscope and give you a correct prediction."

The king agreed. He ordered his minister to make all arrangements for the *Pooja* according to the directions of the astrologer.

The astrologer conducted a *Pooja* in the evening and retired for the night. The king also had a restless night wondering what the astrologer would say the next day.

The day dawned and the second astrologer was promptly present in the court when the king and his entourage arrived. The king seated himself in the throne and gestured the astrologer to proceed.

Just as the previous day, the second astrologer also started his prayers first and opened the box that had the horoscope. He gently placed it on the small platform that had been set in front of him and proceeded to study it doing calculations from time to time. After about half an hour, the astrologer looked up at the king and queen with a smile.

"Oh, Maharajah. The Gods are kind to you. Astrology predicts some good omens in future for you. You will celebrate your sixtieth birthday with great splendour with your whole family with the queen, your sons, and grandsons by your side. Also, your grandsons will rule this kingdom with great pomp and success and be known all over the country as generous and benevolent kings. You are lucky to have such lovable grandsons who will carry your legacy forward."

The king was overjoyed. He ordered celebrations all over his kingdom to celebrate this good news. He rewarded the astrologer well and asked him, "What else would you like to have?"

"Your Majesty, said the astrologer, "Please grant pardon to the first astrologer and free him so that he can return to his kingdom".

The king who felt magnanimous after hearing the good news immediately ordered the first astrologer to be released from prison.

Both the astrologers packed their satchels and left the kingdom together. The first one thanked the second astrologer profusely saying, "But for your recommendation, the king would not have released me and would have kept me a prisoner for a long time. But how did you do it? You know pretty well that all the stars in the king's horoscope were in the most unfavourable positions."

The second astrologer smiled and winked, "It is a matter of communication only my dear friend, he said. My predictions were exactly like yours. But I presented it to the king in a different way."

'How is that. What did you say?", asked the first astrologer.

"I knew that the queen and the king's two sons will die when the king is sixty-two years old. But instead of telling him that bad news, I told him that he will be alive during his sixtieth birthday and will celebrate it in a grand manner with his queens, sons, and grandsons. I did not talk about the tragedy at the age of sixty-two."

"But what about the grandsons?", asked the former.

"Yes, but the grandsons will escape the violent attack on the family and when they grow up, they will rule the kingdom in a very good manner. I was not wrong in that too. I did not mention the death of the queen."

The former nodded in agreement.

"Look here my friend," said the second astrologer smilingly, "Sometimes we have to hide the truth from people, but we should use discretion to mask the truth in a befitting manner."

"Yes, I agree", said the former, "I was indiscreet in answering the king's question and was blunt when I told the truth. I learnt my lesson."

Moral: Sometimes, a bitter truth will have to be couched in nice words of diplomacy.

Shashtiabdapoorthi: It is a religious ceremony celebrating the sixtieth birthday.

Pundit: An expert in a particular subject especially religious scripture

Pooja: A religious prayer / ceremony.

14. Honesty

Thathu", Vijaya said, "Jaya has lost her box of crayons which Appa gave her for Christmas"

I looked at Jaya's face. It seemed that something was troubling her. "What's the problem?", I asked her.

"No, Thathu, I did not lose the box of crayons. I lent it to my friend Tessy in class as she had lost her box of crayons and could not draw a picture for the drawing competition. Vijaya did not know that."

"Good, Jaya", I complimented her smiling, "What you did is a noble deed. But over and above that, you were honest about saying what happened to your box of crayons".

"You have been very honest unlike some of the youngsters who tried to fool the king when he was trying to test their honesty."

"Tell us that story, Thathu", they said, and I began telling them the story about Honesty…

. . . .

Once upon a time there was a king who was just and benevolent. The whole kingdom was fond of him. All his subjects loved and respected him like their own father. The king was nearing seventy years of age and his queen was two years younger to him. But alas, they had no children. The only worry that the king had was as to who would rule his kingdom after the king's death.

The seventieth birthday of the king was celebrated with great pomp and splendour and the king retired to his chambers after all the festivities were over. That night, the king had a strange dream. He saw two angels conversing in the sky. They were talking about him.

"The king is old, "said the first angel, "He may not live long. Whom will he crown as the prince so that he can take over the kingdom's reins when the king is no more".

"From what I gathered," said the second angel, "Only an honest young man from the kingdom who is between twenty and twenty-five years of age can take over the kingdom and run it as benevolently as the king does. If so, the kingdom will be in good hands after the death of the king."

"But are not the courtiers and ministers who surround the king now hypocrites and sycophants. They are dishonest to the core. The king cannot trust any of them with his kingdom. They are all cheats and are only after the king's wealth and not loyal to him at all", said the former angel.

"Yes, quite true," replied the second angel, "These ministers, courtiers or their sons cannot be trusted with the kingdom at all. But I am sure that the intelligent king will find a way to select an honest youth from his kingdom.

Soon both the angels faded away and the king abruptly woke up from sleep.

The king was thoughtful the whole day and by evening had come to a decision as to what to do.

The next day, the king asked all his courtiers and ministers to assemble in his court for an important announcement. Everyone in the court was eager to know what the announcement would be. But not even the chief minister knew what the king was going to announce the next day.

The next morning the king assembled his court and made his proclamation. "I am planning to choose my heir apparent soon. I want all the healthy and able-bodied youth in this kingdom between the ages of twenty and twenty-five to assemble tomorrow morning in the courtyard in front of the palace at eleven o'clock. I will be giving them a task to perform and thereby choose my heir." The congregation was dispersed.

The next day at eleven in the morning there was a large crowd of about a hundred youngsters standing in front of the courtyard. The sons of the king's courtiers and ministers also were among the crowd. The king came in full regalia to inspect the crowd. The youth were asked to stand in rows arranged by the guards.

The king addressed them, "My dear children," the king said, "This is really a contest that I am organizing, but it is very simple and straightforward. I will give each one of you a pot with manure in it. And to each one of you I will give a packet of seeds of the same flower. You must plant the seeds in the pot today and tend to it carefully so that it grows and blooms. Bring the pot to me exactly one month from today at the same time and I will give you, my verdict."

The king retired to his palace and the people were left wondering what the contest was.

"Just growing a flowering plant in a pot and bringing it to the king after one month?", said one minister. "How is the king going to find out his heir apparent by this test?", they wondered among themselves and dispersed. Some even went muttering that the king was obviously senile and out of his senses.

One month flew by.

At the end of one month, the king summoned the same group of young men and asked them to place the pots labelled with their names in the courtyard in rows so that the king could inspect them.

The king came down from his palace. He found that the pots were arranged in neat rows of ten each. The pots held flowers of various colours and hues. Some were red, some pink, some yellow and some orange. They were all exquisite to look at. All the pots that had been distributed had been brought back on the order of the king, without a single exception.

With a smile the king walked amidst the rows carefully inspecting the names on the pots and the beautiful flowers that had been grown in them. He was almost at the end of the last row, when he noticed one pot which was barren with no plant in it. The king raised his eyebrows without a word and the chief minister who was behind him shrugged and pointed out to a young man standing at a distance. The youth was clad in a neat dhoti and was well-built and muscular. He had neat, combed hair and radiated confidence. The king looked at him and the young man looked back straight into the king's eyes. "Is this yours?", the king asked him.

The young man bowed and replied, "Yes, your Majesty, that is my pot".

The king did not say a word. He turned back and walked back to his palace. The chief minister walking behind the king looked at the youth with a sneer.

The king's minister had noted the names of all those who had brought the pots and told them to assemble the next day for the king's final announcement.

The king discretely called two of his trusted spies and asked them to follow the youth who had brought the empty pot and find out more about him. The next day, they reported back to the king saying that the young man and his father who was aged but healthy lived at the edge of the township and the son and father had a small patch of land that they cultivated. They were honest and hardworking people, not bothering anyone and were fending for themselves. The son and the father were very helpful to anyone who was poor and needy.

All the youth had assembled in the courtyard the next day and the king came out of his palace on to the podium. His eyes searched for the youth and found him standing in the last row along with an elderly gentleman- apparently his father. The king whispered to his guard and the guard went post haste and brought both to the front.

The king announced, "I declare that this young man will be the heir to my throne, and I am crowning him prince."

A roar of protests went up from the crowd. "It is unfair", shouted some, "His pot was empty with no plant or flower, ours were full of beautiful blooms".

The king held up his hand. A silence fell on the crowd. "I gave each of you a packet of seeds of the same flowering plant with flowers of the same colour. The seeds had been roasted knowing fully well that they would never sprout. Every one of you cheated by planting some other flowering plant and bringing it here. Only this young man was honest enough to bring back the empty pot as his seeds wouldn't grow!"

A loud groan arose from the crowd.

The youth and the elderly gentleman, who was his father, came and bowed to the king.

"Oh, Majesty, we are honoured", said the father, "You would not recognise me or my son. I am king Randheer of a faraway kingdom. I was defeated and exiled by my enemy and since then have been living in your kingdom incognito. I am glad that you chose my son as the heir to your throne. He is a real prince."

The king was overjoyed to have got a son who was also a prince. "I am extremely happy," he declared, "As a prince you have shown to the world that honesty pays". Saying so, the king embraced the prince.

Moral: Honesty is the best policy

Quote: *"Honesty is the first chapter in the book of wisdom."* Thomas Jefferson

15. The Last Palace

"I have finished all the maths problems that our miss gave me for homework", Jaya said keeping her pen down with a sigh of relief.

I checked her answers cursorily. The last maths problem was simple, but Jaya had made a couple of simple, careless mistakes. "What happened, Jaya", I asked her, "Why is the last problem showing so many careless mistakes? You weren't careful", I chided her.

"No, Thathu, that was the last problem only. So, I did not pay much care when I worked it out", she said listlessly.

"No, Jaya, that attitude is wrong.", I said, "You should show equal interest in all the problems alike. In life too, you must solve all problems with equal gusto. There is no 'last' or 'first' problem in life. It is like the carpenter who built his last palace for the king."

"Oh, Thathu, tell us that story of the carpenter", shouted both together and I began the story of the Last Palace…

. . . .

Once upon a time there was a king in a faraway land which abounded in riches. He was a very generous king. He ruled his kingdom with honesty and his subjects were very loyal to him.

The king had a carpenter who had been working for him for a very long time. The carpenter was an adept in building palaces and his architecture, and deftness were unsurpassed. The carpenter had built many palaces for the king, queen, and the princes during his tenure in the king's court and was getting old. He was also getting careless and becoming grouchier as age advanced.

One day, the carpenter went to the king and said, "Oh, king, I am getting old, and I feel that it is time to retire. You must entrust the job of construction hereafter to one of the younger and worthy carpenters."

"I understand, my dear friend", said the king, "I know you are getting old and want to retire. But not yet, before you leave, I want you to build me one last palace, a small but elegant one putting all the skill that you have at your disposal and make it an excellent abode."

"But your Majesty", said the carpenter, "I was hoping to retire at the end of this month and lead a quiet life in my home."

Not yet", said the king, "You shall build a palace for me before you retire – a beautiful, small, exquisite, and luxurious palace, the last palace. After that I will let you go."

The carpenter was bitter and sullen. He did not want to work anymore, but he could not offend the king either. So, he set about building the palace which the king wanted as his last piece of work.

All his bitterness, anger and annoyance went into his work and made him careless. Instead of choosing the best materials to build the palace, the carpenter chose cheap materials available and was lax in his work. He did not exercise his full skill in the building of the palace. He did not plan the architecture in the excellent way that he used to do previously and did not adorn the walls with the beautiful murals as he used to do in his previous constructions.

In all the previous palaces that the carpenter built, he used to landscape them with beautiful gardens with delightful fountains and magnificent flowering plants and trees. But this time he was not in a mood to design such fascinating gardens. He was working without proper focus, concentration, interest, and dedication in his work.

Finally, the palace was completed, and the carpenter heaved a sigh of relief. The palace was not at all up to his usual standard, as he had not put his mind and heart into his work. It was a structure unworthy of a king, let alone a prince or a minister.

When the palace was completed, the carpenter was summoned to the king's presence as the king was going to declare his retirement. The king, queen and all the courtiers were present there to attend the event.

The king rose and addressed the court. The carpenter was seated in a prominent place of honour in the front row amidst the courtiers. It was a rare honour for a carpenter to be seated in front of the king.

The king came down from his throne, approached the carpenter and hugged him. He said, "You have served me honestly for over forty years and I know that you want to retire and spend the rest of your time in leisure."

A guard approached the king with a plate covered with a silken cloth. The king removed the cloth and there was a plate full of gold coins – a retirement gift for the carpenter. Tears welled up in the carpenter's eyes.

"What a fool I have been", he thought, "the king is honouring me with such a costly gift, and I have been untruthful to him". But he kept quiet.

But the final surprise was yet to come. The king turned to the second guard who stood beside him with a tray and from it removed a small velvet pouch and inside it was the gleaming key to the palace which the carpenter had built as the last palace.

"This is my retirement gift to you, my dear friend", said the king, "The palace which I told you to build was for you and not for me. That was why I wanted you to make it beautiful, luxurious, and exquisite. It will be your home after retirement." With these words, the king handed over the key to the last palace to the carpenter.

The carpenter was flabbergasted. Words failed him. His head hung in shame. He fell at the feet of the king seeking forgiveness for his mean and grouchy behaviour.

Moral: Whatever be your job, do it with sincerity and dedication always. In life there is no 'last problem'.

16. The King's Chief Minister

Amma was sitting at the table. She called out, "Jaya, Vijaya, today I am going to make an orange tea cake. Who is going to help me?"

"I will", shouted both.

Being younger, Amma gave the chance to Vijaya, "Vijaya, go and fetch me the ingredients for making the batter for the cake", she ordered.

Vijaya went to the pantry and came back with a jar of flour. Then she went back again to fetch two eggs. Again, she returned to the pantry to fetch the ingredients one by one.

Seeing this, I laughed. I was sitting at the table sipping coffee and reading a children's book by Ruskin Bond. "Why, Vijaya", I remarked with a smile, "You should have put all the ingredients on one tray and brought it here. You remind me of the king's minister who went ten times out of the palace to find out what the procession outside was."

Jaya who was sitting on the sofa reading a book by Enid Blyton, suddenly appeared, and said, "Thathu, you must tell us that story."

And so, I told the story of the King's Chief Minister…

⋅⋅⋅⋅⋅⋅⋅⋅⋅⋅⋅⋅

Once upon a time there lived a King. He had a very intelligent and efficient Chief minister. The chief minister used to look after all the affairs of the state and used to advise the king on all matters from time to time. The king put his entire faith in the Chief minister and for all matters used to consult the chief minister.

This made the other ministers very jealous. They wanted to be like the chief minister and wanted to attract the king's attention, but the king trusted only the Chief minister and would not heed advice from anyone else.

The other ministers started grumbling and soon this reached the king's ears. He decided to teach the ministers a lesson, at the same time prove the calibre of his chief minister.

One day, the king was in his court along with all the ministers. There was some loud commotion heard from outside the walls of the palace along the adjacent road. The king called one of his ministers, the one who had the maximum grudge against the chief minister and told him, "Go and find out what that commotion outside the palace is about."

The minister came back after a few minutes and said, "Oh, your majesty, there is a marriage procession that is going outside the palace, and they are causing the whole commotion".

"Oh! whose marriage, is it?", the king enquired.

"I did not ask that your majesty", the minister replied. "I'll find out". The minister went out again and returned with the answer, "It is the marriage of a rich businessman's daughter, your majesty".

"Well," asked the king, "Who is the rich businessman? What business does he do?"

The minister went out again and came back with the answer, "His name is Ram Chand. He is in the jewellery business".

"Who is his son marrying?", asked the king.

Again, the minister went out and came back promptly with the reply, "His son is marrying the daughter of another businessman".

"Well," commented the king sarcastically, "You went so many times to find out the details, now wait and see".

The king sent a guard to fetch the chief minister, who was not present in the court at that time. The chief minister came and with all respect bowed before the king. "What did you summon me for, your majesty", asked the chief minister.

"There is some commotion outside the palace walls. Go and find out what it is", said the king.

The chief minister went out and was gone for a long time. He returned after about half an hour and said, "Your majesty, it is the wedding procession of the daughter of a rich businessman named Ram Chand who is living in the Grand Street near the temple. The bridegroom is a youngster named Krishna Kishore who is working in the adjacent kingdom as a teacher in the university. His father is Kishan Chand, who is a leading textile manufacturer in that kingdom. He has three daughters, and this is the eldest daughter. She is eighteen years old and has learnt the art of drawing and painting as a hobby. She also assists her father in the manufacturing business. The marriage will be conducted at the bride's residence tomorrow morning. The *muhurtham* is at eleven o'clock and the bridegroom's party will leave the day after tomorrow taking the bride with them. About five hundred guests have been invited for the ceremony tomorrow."

The king looked at the minister who had gone to enquire previously with contempt. "Do you understand now as to why he is the chief minister, and why you are nowhere near him? When you are sent to enquire about something, you should find out comprehensively, what is it about. Not find out things in bits and pieces superficially.

All the other ministers in the court hung their heads in shame.

Moral: When entrusted any job do it sincerely, truthfully, and completely.

Muhurtham: Auspicious time of the day for the ceremony.

17. The Intelligent Girl

"Thathu," said Jaya one morning to me, "Tell me a story about an intelligent boy or girl"

"What for do you want such a story", I asked her.

"Our class teacher has told us to recite a story about intelligence in our class on Monday. It is my turn this Monday".

"Okay, sure", I said, "I will tell you the story of an intelligent village girl which you can recite in class on Monday". And I told them the story of the Intelligent Girl…

Once upon a time in a village lived a farmer. He had a beautiful daughter who was twenty years old. She had studied in the local school till the 12th standard but owing to financial constraints in the family, could not pursue her studies further. She was a very intelligent girl and was quick on the uptake.

Her father's farming had suffered recently due to the drought and the floods that had followed, and hence, he had taken a large sum of money as loan from the village headman who was a scoundrel and used to cheat and dupe people because of his unscrupulous ways.

Months had rolled by, but as his farming had encountered rough weather, the farmer could not repay the loan on time.

One day the village headman with a couple of his sycophants who were goons came to the farmer's house. He wanted his money back and threatened the farmer with dire consequences if he did not to pay him back his capital with interest.

The farmer was at a loss as to what to tell the village headman, as he did not have the money with him to settle the account. Just then, the young daughter of the businessman came to the room to serve tea to the guests. The village headman stared at her and was enamoured of her beauty. He immediately wanted to marry this girl to his son. His son was a notorious rowdy in the village and was always getting into one or other problems with the police. Everyone feared and avoided him. The village headman hence could not find a suitable bride for his son from among the village folk.

The head man told the farmer, "I will waive your payment if you give your daughter in marriage to my son. If not, you must pay the entire amount within one week. If you don't, I will see that your properties are confiscated, and you are driven out of your house and this village."

The farmer was shocked. He had no words to say. He did not have the money to pay the headman within one week. At the same time, he did not want his charming daughter to marry the headman's son who was a hooligan and a criminal. He was totally at a loss as to what to reply, when his intelligent daughter came to his rescue.

"Papa", she said, "I agree to marry this man's son if our Goddess Durga, gives me permission. We can make the decision in front of the temple which is near the riverbed on Friday morning at 9 o'clock, that being a good *muhurtam*. I will choose the method as to how to decide whether the Goddess favours my marriage with him."

The businessman had nothing to say and was at a loss for words. The girl assured him that all will be well and not to worry. She had a plan in her mind to circumvent this situation.

On Friday, all the village elders were assembled in front of the temple to witness this interesting event. The temple priest had been told about the girl's request to pray to the Goddess to guide her through this test of faith.

The priest brought out a small pouch bag from his pocket. The riverbed where the temple was situated, had a lot of pebbles of various sizes, black ones and white ones strewn all over. The priest told the public, the village headman and his son that he had selected two small pebbles - one black and one white from the riverbed where they stood. Everyone stood on the riverbed on the pebbles and wondered what the test was going to be. The priest said, "After her prayers inside the temple, the girl will come out and with her eyes blindfolded will pick a pebble from the pouch bag. Of the pebbles, one is white and the other black. If she picks the black pebble, she will have to wed the headman's son. If she picks the white pebble, she need not marry him, and the village headman should also write off the interest to be paid by the businessman.

The girl clad in a red saree with a red *bindi* on her forehead, went inside the temple and stood with closed eyes in front of the *sanctum sanctorum* praying silently. After ten minutes, she emerged from the temple and stood before the expectant crowd. The priest tied a cloth over her eyes to prevent her from seeing which pebble she chose. The girl first looked up at the sky with folded hands as if entreating God to guide her and inserted her right hand into the pouch bag held by the priest and picked up a pebble in her clenched fist. She held the pebble between her palms folded in prayer when, she accidentally dropped the pebble on to the riverbed. "Alas", she cried, "the pebble fell from my hands". The priest removed her blindfold.

The priest looked down at the riverbed which was full of black and white pebbles and could not identify the pebble she had dropped. He said, "Since she dropped the pebble which she picked up from the sachet, we shall see what is the colour of the pebble that is left in the sachet. That will tell us which one she picked up."

Everyone brightened at the idea and agreed. The priest put his hand into the satchel and pulled out the remaining pebble. It was black in color. Everyone gave a gasp of surprise.

"The Goddess Durga has spoken", said the priest, "The girl had picked up a white pebble as the remaining one is black. So, she does not have to marry the village headman's son. Also, the farmer should pay back the headman's capital, but the interest should be waived as per the terms of the test."

Everyone cheered. The village headman had no choice but to agree.

The farmer and his daughter thereby were saved from the clutches of the headman and his criminal son. They went home happy. The daughter fell at the feet of the priest and sought his blessing and thanked him.

On the way home, the businessman told his daughter, "My girl, if by any misfortune, you had picked the black pebble, then you would have been condemned to live with that headman's wicked son for life according to the agreement.

The daughter laughed aloud, "No papa, she said, it would never have happened because, yesterday evening, I came to the temple and met the priest and told him my predicament. I told him to keep two black pebbles in the small pouch bag instead of one white and one black. I deliberately dropped the pebble on to the riverbed so that no one will know which one I picked up from the pouch. The priest helped me in this."

The farmer was surprised by his daughter's ingenuity and told her, "You are indeed a wise girl to overcome such a problem and teach the village headman a lesson".

Moral: Intelligence and wit can solve many problems that cannot be solved by other means.

Durga: A Hindu Goddess who is protective of her devotees and removes evil from the world.

Muhurtam: An auspicious time

Bindi: A vermilion mark worn on the forehead by Hindu women.

Sanctum Sanctorum: The innermost part of a temple where the idol of the God is kept.

18. The King and the Eagle

"Hi, orange juice", said Vijaya and took the glass of orange liquid that was lying on the worktable in the kitchen.

She was about to drink it when Amma saw it and shouted, Viji, don't you drink that. That is my Isapgol powder for constipation!".

Everyone had a hearty laugh at this. "Vijaya, if you'd have drunk that, tomorrow morning you will not come out of the toilet", Jaya teased her.

Vijaya felt completely humiliated and hurt. With a sullen look on her face, she turned to go to her room.

I stopped her and just to pacify her, said, "Vijaya, have you heard of the story of the king who went to the forest to hunt?"

Vijaya's face brightened, "Thathu, tell us that story now itself".

And I began the story of the King and the Eagle…

. . . .

There was a king who ruled his kingdom wisely. Near his kingdom there was a forest. The king's pastime was hunting. He used to go during weekends into the forest and hunt for small animals and birds. His minister and courtiers used to accompany him during these hunting trips. The king and the minister used to enjoy these hunting trips very much.

Once the king went deep into the forest and lost his way. His courtiers and guards who had accompanied him got separated from him and were left behind and the king became alone. The forest was quite dark and even sunlight hardly penetrated the forest through the overhanging foliage of the huge trees around him. Furthermore, heavy clouds forewarning impending rain had gathered and made the area darker than before. The king felt scared as he did not know the way out of this thick forest. He had been walking all day and felt tired and thirsty. The king started wandering in search of water to quench his thirst. Soon he found a small pond amid a clearing in the jungle. He stopped there, but it was too dark for him to see what lay around the pond and the water in it.

Being very thirsty, the king placed his bow and arrow near him and bent down to drink some water with his cupped hands. Just then, an eagle which had been sitting on a branch of a nearby tree, swooped down on him and attacked him. The king could not drink the water as he tried to ward off the eagle's attack.

He chased the eagle away and it went back to its perch on the tree. After the eagle had gone, he went back to the pond and knelt beside it again to drink water from the pond, when the eagle swooped down and attacked him a second time. This happened four times.

Finally, the king lost his patience and picked up his bow and arrow. He took careful aim and shot an arrow at the eagle. With a loud shriek, the eagle fell from its perch, struggled for some time, and died.

With a sigh of relief, the king bent down and took a handful of water in his cupped hands. Just then, the clouds cleared, and the sun shone through a clearing in the sky. The king saw the water clearly now as the sun was reflected in the water in the pond. To his horror, he found a large snake, a King Cobra which had died in the pond. Its carcass was rotting in the water. The poison from the snake had seeped into the water in the pond.

The king knew that if he had drunk that water and washed his face and mouth with it, he would have died. Only then did he see that around the pond there were carcasses of a deer, a fox, and a mongoose – they had died after drinking the water in the pond.

To his dismay, the king realised that the eagle that had attacked him was trying to save him from definite death and was doing a noble gesture. But the king without realising this had hastily killed the poor bird. He regretted his action.

The king understood that even in the face of adversity, one should think twice before taking any action and avoid doing anything impulsively.

Moral: Impulsiveness may lead to disaster. Think before you act.

19. The Diamond Merchant and the Beggar

Thathu", said Vijaya bringing an old dilapidated hard cover album which was perhaps fifty or sixty years old. "Shall I throw it in the trash can? She asked, "It is tattered and dirty."

"Wait I said", before discarding anything, verify it twice whether it has any important items or pictures. This album seems very old. Let us have a look."

I placed the dilapidated album on the flat surface of the table and turned the pages one by one with great care. Imagine my surprise when I saw well-preserved pictures of my childhood, my parents, uncles, and aunts. It was a treasury of reminiscences.

I summoned the kids to my side and showed them the old black and white snaps, "This is my mother, that is your great-grandma and this your great-grandpa. See how smart they look."

We spent half an hour reminiscing about my relatives and finally straightened up with a sigh coming back to the reality of today. "We'll scan these photos and preserve them forever", I said, "That way your children also can see them after a few decades."

Never throw away old things without verifying what they are, or you will end up like the diamond merchant and the beggar."

Instantly, the kids pounced on me, "Thathu, tell us that story".

And I began the story of the Diamond merchant and the Beggar…

. . . .

In a village in a remote kingdom, lived a beggar who had been poor from childhood. He had no house to live. He did not remember who his parents were. His only possession was a bundle of tattered clothes, a blanket, and a wooden casket which his father had left him. The casket contained some items used by his father, some tattered clothes worn by his father, a faded photograph, a broken mirror, and a dog-eared copy of the Bhagavad Gita.

The beggar used to live in the temple *mandap* and used to eat the offerings which the priest gave him after the daily *pooja*. Occasionally, the village folk used to give him their old clothes, bed sheets or blankets. At night he used to sleep in the temple *mandap* resting his head on the wooden casket which he used instead of a pillow.

The beggar used to help people around the village. In the morning he used to get up and go around the village doing small chores for the village folk. He used to fetch water from the common well in the village for the women folk, help with gardening for the elderly, carry vegetables and groceries home when the villagers went shopping – and the like. He was liked by all the village folk as he was a calm and docile person. He never used to beg for alms and the villagers would willingly give him food and clothes when he helped them in their day-to-day activities.

One afternoon, as the beggar was resting beneath the banyan tree near the temple, a large car came to a stop near him. As there was no one nearby, the gentleman sitting in the back of the car got down and approached the beggar. He seemed to be a cultured man wearing a *dhoti* and a *turban* and was typically dressed like a businessman.

Seeing no one else around, he approached the beggar and asked, "tell me which is the house of Pattabhiram here. I have come from a faraway town to see him".

The beggar knew who Pattabhiram was. He was a famous jeweller in the village and owned a large jewellery shop near the king's palace.

"I know the place", said the beggar, "It is nearby here". I will take you there. The beggar led the way on foot and the gentleman followed him.

The beggar used to go the jeweller's house frequently to help them with various chores and was familiar with their mansion. He left the gentleman at the gate and returned to the shade of the banyan tree for his afternoon nap.

In the evening, as the beggar had his bath in the temple pond as was his wont and finished his prayers in the temple, he saw the gentleman returning from the jeweller's mansion. The gentleman stopped in front of the banyan tree, took out a ten rupee note from his pocket and gave it to the beggar. "Thanks for your help in leading me to Pattabhi's house."

With these words, the gentleman turned to leave when his eyes fell on the wooden casket. He turned back and asked, "Shall I ask you something, if I may, who gave you this wooden casket?"

"Oh, this", the beggar replied, "This was my father's. My parents died in a fire in our home when I was a very small boy, and this was the only thing left after the fire destroyed everything in our house."

"May I see it?", asked the gentleman. He seemed to be curious. "Can you open this for me? I would like to inspect the casket."

"Sure", said the beggar and opened the casket to reveal the contents- tattered clothes, a broken mirror, an old Bhagavad Geetha book and the faded photograph. He dumped all this on to the ground and held out the casket to the gentleman.

The gentleman's eyes fell on the photograph, and he picked it up and squinted at it. Suddenly, his eyes lit up with surprise. He quickly picked up the dog-eared book and opened it. There in a clear handwriting was the name Vishnu Datta.

"Is this your father's photo?", asked the gentleman.

"Yes", replied the beggar, "But I don't remember him at all".

"My God!" exclaimed the gentleman, "Vishnu Dutta was a friend of mine. He was a jeweller staying near my village. He and his wife were killed in a fire which engulfed his home long ago and his only son went missing."

"Is this your father's casket?", asked the businessman. "If so, there is something you should see." The gentleman fumbled around the bottom of the casket and released a tiny catch and the bottom opened to reveal many little silken pouches inside. The gentleman opened one pouch and out fell ten sparkling diamonds!

The other pouches also held various gemstones – rubies, amethysts, sapphires, pearls and many more.

The beggar watched the whole scene with wonder.

Little did he realise that all these years he had been lying on a very rich treasure without realising that he was rich.

The gentleman led the beggar to his car and told him, "You may come with me and join me in the business. You are a rich man and no longer a beggar."

Moral:	There are many unrecognised riches in our lives. Occasionally luck unveils these treasures to us. Remember, Old is Gold.

Bhagavad Gita: A religious scripture of the Hindus.

Mandap: A raised platform, used for worship or religious ceremonies

Dhoti: A garment worn by males in South India, a long cloth tied at the waist and extending to cover the ankles.

Turban: A long head dress worn by men in India a long cloth worn around the head by swathing a length of linen or silk.

20. The Pet Mongoose

"Thathu, Thathu", shouted Vijaya, "There is a rabbit here in the garden and it is bleeding from the mouth! I think it has bitten some other rabbit or other animal."

I went near the rabbit in the garden only to find that it was munching on a piece of beet root which my daughter had thrown away. It was not blood.

"Don't jump to hasty conclusions, Vijaya", I chided her. Do you know what happened to the pet mongoose which had blood on its teeth?"

"Oh, Thathu", the children pleaded, "Tell us that story".

And I began the story of the Pet Mongoose...

． ． ． ． ． ． ． ． ． ． ． ．

In a village in India lived a woman with her ten-month old baby son. The woman's husband had passed away three months ago in an accident, and she lived in a small house with her baby son and a maid. The woman used to go to work in a nearby factory during daytime entrusting the baby to the maid, who used to take very good care of the baby.

After the mother went to work the maid used to bathe the baby, feed it with gruel made of millets and put it to sleep in the cradle which hung from a beam in the roof.

The woman also had a pet dog and a pet mongoose which she had been rearing for a long time. The dog used to accompany her to the factory and return in the evening with her. The mongoose used to run about in the house and chase away any small rodents that used to come near like rats, squirrels etc.

On a bright sunny day, the mother left the child in the cradle and told the maid that she was going to the factory early as she had a lot of work that day. The child was fast asleep when she left, and the maid was busy in the kitchen cooking.

Unfortunately, there was a sudden strike in the factory that day when the labourers and other factory workers struck work. Hence, by noon the woman returned home. The sun was shining bright, and the day was quite hot.

The woman opened the door of the house with the key that she carried in her purse, when she heard a squealing sound and the loud wail of her baby. She rushed to the bedroom where the baby was lying in the cradle and found the mongoose standing near the cradle in the room with blood dripping from its teeth. The baby was wailing in the cradle and there was blood in its clothes, the baby's blanket, and bedsheets. Blood was dripping on to the floor from the edge of the cradle.

Immediately the woman thought that the mongoose had bitten her baby and hence the baby was crying. In a fit of rage, she beat the mongoose with the umbrella which she had in her hand and the mongoose ran away with a whimper.

The woman ran to the cradle and picked up the baby in her arms. The baby's clothes were soaked in blood, but it stopped crying the moment its mother caressed it. On careful inspection, the woman found that the baby was uninjured, and the blood was not that of the baby. she looked amidst the clothes in the cradle and to her horror found a dead snake – a poisonous cobra within folds of the bed sheet. The snake was dead and had bled.

Only then, did the truth dawn on her. The mongoose had seen the snake in the baby's cradle and had jumped in to save the baby. In the tussle between the mongoose and the cobra, it had managed to bite the cobra to death.

"Oh, what a fool I have been", moaned the woman, "I suspected the mongoose of having bitten my dear baby. I was too hasty to hit the mongoose".

Meanwhile, the maid who had been in the rest room taking a bath ran into the room and found the mother and baby safe.

The mother handed the baby to the maid and ran outside into yard where she saw the mongoose lying dead in a pool of blood. The snake had bitten the mongoose and in trying to save the baby, the mongoose had given up its life.

The woman's cries of repentance echoed on the walls of the house. But her pet mongoose had been lost forever. She cried lamenting her hasty decision in beating the faithful mongoose.

Moral: Never take any hasty decision when you are upset. Look before you leap.

21. The Lazy Officers

"Thathu, I want you to help me do the math lessons. You do it for me", Jaya said, "I find it difficult to do the maths problems."

"Look here, Jaya", I said, "You have to do the problems yourself. I cannot do them for you. Everyone must do their work themselves. You are your own friend, and you can become your own enemy if you are not careful."

"Haven't you heard the story of the Lazy officers in the government office?" I asked.

"Thathu", shouted both kids together, "Tell us that story, Thathu".

And I began telling the story of the Lazy Officers in a government office…

．．．．．．．．．．．

Once upon a time, there was a government office. As usual matters used to move in this office very slowly and everyone in the office from the lowest clerk to the highest officers were lazy and their smartness lay only on the first of every month when they had to collect their salaries. No amount of coaxing and cajoling could get them to improve and the chairman and managing director of the office found it very difficult to make these men work.

One day, a new office manager was appointed as the chief in this office. He was a very straightforward man and a perfectionist who expected others to be like him. He watched all of them work lackadaisically in the office and within a week or two realised that all his subordinates were indifferent and listless in their jobs. He decided to give them a shock treatment.

One morning he came into the office with a smile and distributed *laddus* to all the staff in the office.

What is this celebration for?" asked all the employees.

The officer said, "I have identified a few of you whom I will be dismissing at the end of the month. But before that I will give you a warning. In the next room, I have placed a framed photograph of the one person who is most lazy and lethargic in his work. One by one all of you may go and see that photograph in the room, come back to your workplaces and continue your work without discussing anything among yourselves."

He continued, "Your work will be assessed in the next fifteen days and the results will be sent to the chairman at the end of that period, I will be carrying out my promise and in consultation with the Chairman, be dismissing the inefficient and irresponsible persons."

The officer sat down at his desk with a smile.

One by one, each of the staff member went into the room and came back looking ashen and trembling. They went to their seats in silence and continued their work without interruption and gossip. At the end of the day, each one went home wondering who would be axed at the end of the month.

Everyone in the office worked diligently for the next two weeks. The efficiency of the office remarkably improved. At the end of two weeks the Managing director came for an inspection of the office. He was astounded to find all the staff working silently and diligently. All the files that had to be completed had been done and there was no pending work to be done at the end of the month.

The Managing Director called the new office manager and asked him, "What miracle have you worked in this office. All the previous office chiefs here had failed to correct these staff, but you have single-handed done this wonderful transformation. How did you do it?"

The new office chief explained to him about the locked room where he had made this change possible and told him about the framed photograph. With a mischievous smile the manager opened the adjacent room and led the Managing Director into that room.

There on a table in the centre of the room stood a large, framed mirror and a large placard with the following quotation.

You, yourself are your friend

You, yourself are your enemy

Only you can elevate and improve yourself

Only you can deprave yourself.

Bhagavad Gita. Ch. 6, Verse 5.

Now, my dear staff, it is up to you to decide who you want to be. I shall wait till the end of this month to take my decision on whom to sack. – Chief Officer.

The Managing Director came out of the room with a broad smile and slapped the officer in his back. "Well done, you have done the impossible. I appreciate you"

Moral: Improving oneself or debasing oneself depends solely on the individual and not on any external factor or person. We can be our own enemy, or we can be a friend to ourselves.

Laddu: A sweet made of flour and sugar made into balls.

22. The Story of the Earth

All of us together went to a park on Saturday evening. There was a nice trekking path there and we enjoyed trekking through the dense growth of trees and plants. Vijaya and Jaya entertained themselves by plucking the wildflowers and some leaves from the plants and bushes for their dry leaves and dry flower collection.

"Why are they growing all these plants in this park?", asked Jaya, "They are not of any use to anyone. These tall trees don't seem to have any edible fruits either. Why did God create all these trees if they are of no use to us?"

"Don't say like that", I corrected her. "Do you know that once upon a time man became very arrogant and destroyed Nature without caring for the trees and plants and then Bhoomi Devi, the Goddess of the Earth got angry?"

"Thathu, Thathu," said both in unison, tell us that story.

And sitting on the bench in the park, I told them the Story of The Earth…

. . . .

Long ago, there was a King named Prithu who ruled the seven continents of the earth. He was a virtuous king always cherishing the welfare of his subjects. He was honest and straight forward, but wherever he saw injustice, he objected to it and raised his voice against it.

His subjects had all the comforts of life and gradually became greedy and arrogant. They destroyed nature and all the trees and plants in the kingdom without any discrimination. They polluted all the waters in the rivers and ponds in the kingdom and failed in their regular duties. They never bothered about the environment and did not heed the prudent advice of the sages and elders in the community.

Seeing this, the Goddess of the Earth (**Bhoomi Devi)** got extremely angry and decided to teach them a lesson. Gradually, she altered the climate and the vegetation in the kingdom and made the earth parched and barren. The rivers, streams and ponds became dry. The land was arid. People and animals started dying of thirst. Lack of rains made the fields scorched and cracked. No cultivation was possible. The reckless felling of trees in the forest caused a decrease in rains. Severe food shortage ensued. Cattle and birds died en masse. The whole earth reeked of death and destruction. The heat was unbearable. There was famine everywhere.

All the subjects suffered, man, animals, and birds alike. They all went to the King Prithu and voiced their complaint.

The king decided to wage war on Bhoomi Devi and get her to restore all that she had withdrawn into herself. He went in search of the goddess. Knowing that the king was in pursuit, the goddess changed her form into that of a cow and tried to escape. The king pursued her and ultimately overpowered her. Knowing that king Prithu may enslave her, the goddess apologised to the king and promised to restore everything back to normal. She told the king to milk whatever he required from her udder.

The king with the help of many gods and sages got all the nature's bounties from the goddess – Agriculture, Rainfall, abundant flora and fauna, minerals and precious stones and metals from the deep bowels of the earth, and everything that we see in this earth today.

The Goddess Bhoomi Devi also promised the king that, "If you nurture and protect me, I will give whatever you want in plenty from Nature".

From that day, man started cultivation, animals and birds found their food in Nature, rains were plenty and timely, flowers yielded honey, the bowels of the earth yielded precious metals like gold, silver and platinum and other metals like iron. Also, precious stones like rubies, amethysts, topazes, opals, and many others were born from Mother Earth.

When man takes proper care of Nature, Nature too will take care of man and provide all that he needs.

Moral: Nature provides for us provided we nurture it. Do not destroy Nature indiscriminately as it will be end of human civilization on this earth.

Bhoomi Devi: The Goddess of the Earth.

23. The Foolish Donkey

"See Thathu, all of them are waving at me", shouted Vijaya when we were sitting in the park on a bench.

I turned and saw a group of teenagers waving in our direction. I was not sure that they were waving at us, and I looked behind us and there stood another group of teenagers. The former was waving to them, not to us. I pointed this out to Vijaya and said, "Don't be carried away by mere appearances, first you should have verified whether they were waving at you. This is what happened to the foolish donkey."

"Thathu", piped up Vijaya and Jaya, "tell us that story".

And I told them the story of the Foolish Donkey…

. . . .

In a village there lived a washerman. He used to take the clothes to be washed to the river daily and wash them and bring them back. He used to dry them and iron them and deliver the clothes to the homes of his customers without fail. The villagers were pleased with his services and rewarded him handsomely for his services.

The washerman had a donkey which carried all the clothes on its back to and from the riverbank. He used to feed the donkey some grass and grains, but most of the time, he often let the donkey out into the open when it used to go into the fields and gardens of other farmers and eat whatever it obtained from there.

The farmers and the gardeners in the village were fed up with the donkey and constantly used to complain to the washerman that his donkey was gobbling up their grass, produce, fruits and vegetables from their farms and gardens. However, they could not antagonise the washerman as he was the sole washerman in the whole village and all of them, especially the businessmen and politicians were dependent on him for getting their clothes washed and ironed. On the contrary, they would vent their anger on the donkey and beat it with sticks whenever it strayed into their garden or farm. The children also used to throw stones at the donkey to chase it away from their gardens. The donkey used to feel sad that despite its working hard for the washerman, the villagers beat it mercilessly. Every evening, the donkey used to weep when it was tied up in the washerman's shed feeling self-pity.

That year the village elders decided to celebrate the festival of Lord Ganesh (the Ganesh Chaturthi) in a pompous manner and for this they needed a clay idol of the Lord. On enquiry they found out that there was no one in that village who could make the idol. They decided to go to a nearby town and buy the idol from there as there were plenty of craftsmen in that town who could make the idols of Lord Ganesh for the festival.

But the problem was in bringing the idol back to the village. They decided to approach the washerman and seek his help.

"As we have to bring the idol from the town, we need your donkey to carry it back from the village for us", the elders said, approaching the washerman one day in his house.

"By all means", said the washerman, "I will lend you my donkey for such a noble task and do it for free. You don't have to pay me anything for that. I will personally accompany you with the donkey to the town and bring back the idol."

The day arrived when they had to go to the town to buy the idol and bring it back. The washerman got up very early at daybreak and took his donkey to the river and gave it a good scrub bath. Then he smeared *Kumkum* and *Chandan* on its forehead, as it was going on a 'sacred' mission. As an afterthought he also put a garland of sweet-smelling jasmine flowers around its neck.

The donkey felt that it was some important day for it, and the people of the village were honouring it. It started feeling proud and self-important. It held its head high in front of the villagers as if to say, "See, how important I am to be washed and decorated like this.

The washerman and the village elders along with the donkey set off to the nearby town to purchase the idol of Lord Ganesh and bring it back before sundown. Within three hours, they reached the town and the workshop of the idol-maker. After selecting the idol, which was three feet tall, they set out to return to their village. The idol was secured to the back of the donkey and was well fastened with ropes.

On the way, they rested to take food from a restaurant. The donkey also was well fed by the villagers as it was carrying a 'sacred' consignment. All the people on the way crowded around the donkey to have a glimpse of the beautiful idol of Lord Ganesh. Some even prostrated before the idol and paid obeisance to the Lord with folded hands. Some waved incense sticks before the Lord. This continued all along the way and people were flocking around the donkey when they entered the outskirts of their village. Some even fed sweetmeats to the donkey as it was carrying Lord Ganesh on its back!

All along the donkey felt pompous and conceited thinking that the whole respect and reverence that the people were showing was for it. Little did the donkey realise that the people were respecting and venerating the idol and not the donkey. But the donkey never realised that.

The whole night, the donkey was dreaming that it had acquired some greatness and people respected it. But the next day, when the haughty donkey went to the fields and gardens of the villagers to graze in them, it was received with the same beatings that it used to get previously.

Moral: Respect is given to some people only if they are occupying an important position or chair. Do not be carried away by false pretences.

Lord Ganesh: The Elephant-headed God in Hindu Mythology

Chaturthi: The fourth day after the New Moon. Celebrated as a festival to Lord Ganesh. Also called Ganesh Chaturthi.

Kumkum: Red turmeric powder used to make a red mark on forehead by Hindu Ladies.

Chandan: Sandalwood paste smeared on the forehead by Hindus.

24. The Fox, the Cat, and the Tortoise

"I know how to solve this math problem in three different ways", said Jaya with an air of superiority, "It is easy to do".

"Okay then", I challenged her. "Do it in any one way and show me".

She took a long time thinking and then completed the assignment. But the answer was wrong.

I smiled and said, "Jaya, you said that you knew how to solve this problem in three different ways, but you have made a mistake even in the one single way in which you solved it. It reminds me of the story of the fox, the cat and the tortoise".

No sooner had I completed my sentence, than the kids pounced on me, "Thathu, tell us that story".

And I told them the story of the Fox, the Cat, and the Tortoise…

. . . .

In a jungle by the side of a river, lived a fox, a cat, and a tortoise. They were good friends and used to meet daily to talk about various things. The fox used to bring the carcasses of small animals that it had hunted to feed the cat and cabbage and lettuce leaves for the tortoise. Sometimes the cat brought cauliflower, fruits, and vegetables for the tortoise for the tortoise was a strict vegetarian.

They used to be jovial friends and shared their meals and there was good camaraderie among them.

The fox however, always felt a bit superior as it was bigger in size and prided itself on its cleverness and wit. Occasionally, it was given to boasting about its exploits and how it escaped from its enemies like the python and the tiger.

One day, their discussion centred on how to escape if one is suddenly attacked by an enemy animal. Each of them started telling how they would escape such an attack.

The cat said, "I have only one way of escaping, I will scamper and climb up the nearest tree available and usually it is enough for me to escape from most of the enemies. This is because I am small but my swiftness in the face of danger helps me escape using this one and only trick that I know of."

The tortoise said, "Friends, you know that I am a slow creature and can never run. I have only one way of escaping my enemies and that is by withdrawing my limbs and head into my hard carapace shell so that an enemy cannot do anything to me and usually leaves me alone. That is the only trick I know to escape my enemy".

The fox laughed scornfully. "Ho, Ho, I am quick-witted and clever and know one hundred tricks to outwit the enemy. There is no time to elaborate all of them but suffice it to say that whenever there is an attack by an enemy, I devise the appropriate strategy to escape the attack and overcome the assault".

The words of the fox that knew a hundred tricks made the cat and the tortoise envious, but given their size and small stature, they could not compete with the cunning and quick-witted fox. They nodded in agreement and praised the fox for its repertoire of wits.

One day as they were sharing the food brought by the fox and the cat, they heard a loud roar from the jungle and immediately recognised it to be that of the wicked tiger that roamed the area. The roar was informative of the fact that the tiger was in search of a prey to satisfy its hunger. The sound of the roar was very nearby and seemed only a few feet away.

Within minutes, they could smell the spoor of the tiger. Soon they saw the tiger break out through the bushes beyond them and were frozen with fear.

But the cat gathering its senses quickly, clambered up the nearest tree and reached a top branch where the tiger could not reach it. The tortoise immediately withdrew into its shell and curled up inside. The tiger walked around it a couple of times and as it could not do anything, left it alone.

The tiger's attention now fell on to the fox. The fox was still contemplating as to which out of its hundred strategies to adopt to escape from the tiger, when with one swipe of its giant paw the tiger killed the fox.

Moral: It is not important how much you know, but the important fact is how practical is your knowledge to help you in day-to-day life.

25. Yudhishtra and the Yaksha

Jaya came bounding from school one day, "Amma, Thathu, we are having a quiz program in school next Friday afternoon. Attractive prizes will be given to the winners. Our miss announced it in class today."

"Very good", Amma said, "How are you going to prepare your general knowledge for the quiz program? Ask Thathu to help you".

"Thathu, Thathu", Jaya came running to me, will you help me prepare for the quiz program?"

"Sure, dear", said I, "I will help you prepare and conduct a rehearsal for the quiz program for you. By the way do you know who conducted the first quiz program in ancient times?"

"There was no quiz program in ancient times as there was no TV and there were no quiz masters", Jaya answered demurely thinking that TV and Internet were essential for a quiz program.

"You are wrong said I. In the Mahabharatha, there is a story that Yudhishtra was quizzed by a Yaksha when he was in the forest.

"Thathu, tell us that story", clamoured the kids and I began telling the story of Yudhishtra and the Yaksha…

. . . .

The Pandavas were five in number and their cousins, the Kauravas numbered a hundred. The Pandavas were often tormented by the Kauravas mainly because the Kauravas wanted the kingdom which the Pandavas ruled. Consequently, by deceit, the Kauravas snatched the kingdom and banished the Pandavas to the forest for thirteen years.

This story happened during one of their exploits in the forest.

Once, the Pandavas were out hunting when the climate was very hot and humid. The sun was at its peak in the sky. The Pandavas felt very thirsty and sent the youngest of them in search of water. He went around and soon chanced upon a pond with pellucid water surrounded by plenty of sweet-smelling flowering plants.

He bent down to drink the crystal-clear water when he heard a disembodied voice from around him say "Stop, do not drink the water". He raised his head but saw no one around. Again, he cupped his hands to drink the water when the voice announced, "Hey, mortal, answer my questions and then drink the water as this pond belongs to me. If you defy me, you will die."

The youngest brother looked all around again but saw no one anywhere. Ignoring the warning, he took a mouthful of the cool water and immediately fell dead by the side of the pond.

Seeing that his brother hadn't returned, Yudhishtra sent the next brother to investigate. The same fate befell him, and he drank the water without answering any of the questions and fell dead. This continued till Yudhishtra sent all his four brothers and none returned. Very upset, Yudhishtra himself went in search of them. To his horror, he found all his four brothers dead beside the pool but there was no external injury on any of their bodies. Wanting to find out who caused this, Yudhishtra decided to quench his thirst before seeking the enemy.

The voice immediately spoke up. "Yudhishtra, answer my questions before drinking the water, or else, you will also die like your brothers"

"Who are you?", asked Yudhishtra.

"I am a *Yaksha* in charge of this forest and the pond and you cannot defy my orders", the voice answered.

Yudhishtra could not decide from where this disembodied voice came, but he answered, "Oh, mysterious spirit, I am unable to see you. Come forward into the open and fight me if you can. But I will answer your questions."

Well then", the voice said, "Tell me What is heavier than the earth?"

"One's mother is heavier than the earth because she bears you after nine long months and carries you through thick and thin."

The voice continued, "What is higher than the mountains?"

"One's father is higher than the mountains as he cares for you, nurtures you, educates you and makes you fit to work in this world.'

"What is faster than the wind?"

"The mind is faster than the wind because it can travel anywhere in a moment"

"What are more numerous than blades of grass on earth?"

"Worries of man are more numerous than the of blades of grass."

"Who is the friend of a traveller?"

"A friend of a traveller is his companion.

"Who is the friend of one who is ill?"

"The physician is the friend of one who is ill."

"Who is the friend of a dying man".

"Charity that he has done during life is the friend of a dying man."

"What, if renounced, makes a person lovable?"

"Renouncing Pride makes a person lovable."

"When does one become really wealthy."

"One becomes really wealthy when he renounces Desire."

"When does one become happy?"

"One becomes happy when one renounces Avarice."

"Which enemy of man is invincible?"

"Anger is the invincible enemy of man."

"Which disease of man is incurable?"

"Greed in the incurable disease of man."

"Who is a Noble man?"

"He who is passionate about the well-being of all creatures is Noble."

"Who is an Ignoble man?"

"One who is merciless is ignoble."

"Who is the truly happy man?"

"He who has no debts is a truly Happy man."

"What is the greatest wonder of all in the world?"

"Every day, we see people dying all around us. Still man thinks that he is eternal and wants to live forever. This is the greatest wonder on earth."

"Well done, Yudhishtra," the voice said, "You have answered all my questions correctly and to my utter satisfaction". Saying this, the voice took a human form. For it was none other than *Yama* the God of Death who had spoken to Yudhishtra and quizzed him.

"I wanted to meet you and test your depth of knowledge and hence I conducted this little drama. I will restore to life all your brothers." Then, Yama restored all of them to life. The Pandavas bowed before Lord Yama and paid obeisance to them, quenched their thirst and returned.

Moral: The answers to the quiz themselves are morals to be learned.

Pandavas: A clan of five brothers (Read the Mahabharata)

Kauravas: Cousins to the Pandavas. A hundred brothers.

Yaksha: A benevolent, but sometimes mischievous, capricious spirit in Indian Mythology said to be in association with forests, treasures, and water.

26. Deafness

Amma was shouting, "Jaya, Vijaya, where are both of you. Come down for dinner at once, it is getting late".

Despite calling two or three times, there was no response from the children who were upstairs in their room watching an Avatar cartoon.

Finally, Amma went up a few steps and called to them when they heard her and came downstairs for dinner.

"Are you guys deaf or what?", Amma was annoyed.

"We answered you", groaned the kids, "You did not hear us".

To defuse the situation, I said, "You kids are like the wife who did not hear what the husband asked."

"Ah, Thathu, tell us that story while we are having our dinner of Dosas and sambhar", said the kids and I told them the story of the wife who was taken to the doctor by the concerned husband for her "Deafness" …

· · · · · · · · · · · ·

Once upon a time there was a man and wife. The man used to love his wife very much and they had been married for forty years. They lived in a small house in the outskirts of the town. Their children were grown up and were living in a far-off place.

One day, the husband took the wife to a doctor, an ENT surgeon, for a check-up because the husband wanted an opinion regarding his wife's hearing. The surgeon was a leading physician in the town and was very much liked by the townsfolk.

The doctor walked into the consultation room and immediately the husband started speaking in a loud voice. The doctor gestured him to reduce his voice and speak softer.

"Sir, my wife has become deaf over the past one week. I don't know why. Will you please examine her and come to a decision regarding her hearing defect?"

Okay nodded the doctor. He did not speak anything. "How did you know that your wife was deaf?", asked the doctor facing the husband.

"Yesterday my wife was cooking in the kitchen," said the husband, "I was in the next room and came to the door and asked her what she was cooking. She did not reply and continued to cook without bothering to answer me."

All the while the wife kept quiet beside the husband and was smiling.

"What I did", said the husband, "I stood about fifty feet behind her as she was facing the kitchen stove and asked the same question as to what she was cooking. Then I moved forward to forty feet and asked her. Then I moved forward to thirty feet behind her and finally ten feet. All the while I was asking the same question. She never answered me. That is when I concluded that she was deaf."

The doctor looked at the wife and raised his eyebrows.

The wife answered, "Sir he asked the same question five times standing behind me, and without turning around and I answered him all five times as the food could be burnt if I am distracted. I am not the person who is deaf", she said smiling. "I agreed to come with him to consult you as that was the only way I could bring him to you for consultation."

The doctor understood who was deaf.

Moral: Don't always blame the other person for any faults. The fault may really be your own.

Dosa: A thin Pancake made of fermented batter of rice and lentils.

Sambhar: Vegetable stew made with lentils and vegetables, taken along with Dosa.

27. Karna, the Philanthropist

When the children had come to India to live with us for the vacation, they were exposed to the life in India unlike that in the United States. One evening, when my wife had finished the cooking for the night, a poor beggar woman in tattered clothes approached our front door asking for alms. "Amma", she pleaded, "I have not eaten for two days, please give me something to eat".

My daughter, out of pity for the poor woman asked the woman to wait in the patio in the rear of the house and brought some food in a plate and placed it in front of her along with a glassful of water. The woman squatted on the floor and eagerly gulped down the food. After finishing her meals, she said, "Amma, God will bless you and your children. You have given me the greatest alms of all, 'Annadanam'. I cannot forget your generosity. My stomach is full, and I feel contented."

Amma, sent her on her way giving her a couple of her old sarees to wear. The woman left showering blessings on Amma.

The children were watching all this with wonder from the door of the patio. They had never seen such a scene in the U.S. When the woman left, they asked my daughter, "Why Amma was this woman so much satisfied and showered so many blessings on you when all you did was give her some food. You never gave her any money at all."

"Yes kids", Amma said, "Giving food to the hungry is the greatest charity that you can do. No amount of money or gold can satisfy hunger. Only food can satisfy hunger. Go and ask Thathu to tell you the story of Karna who was a philanthropist. He had told me the story when I was a kid like you."

And thus, I told the kids the story of Karna, the Philanthropist…

. . . .

Karna was a king of a small kingdom named Anga. He was a very generous king. Anybody coming to him with any request was never turned back. He used to donate anything that the person asked for. He lavished, gold, precious stones, land, and cattle to anyone coming with a request for alms.

There is legend regarding him that one stormy day with floods all around the kingdom, one poor villager came to him with a request. "Oh, mighty king," he said, "I have no firewood to heat my house and cook my food. All the firewood and the trees have been rendered soggy and wet by the heavy rains. My paddy fields are completely submerged under water. Please help me to get some firewood".

Karna ordered his chief minister to get firewood available anywhere in the kingdom and give it to the poor villager. The chief minister immediately ordered his henchmen to go in search of firewood to be given to the villager.

After a long search, they came back and said, "Oh your majesty, there is no dry firewood available anywhere in the kingdom. Everything is drenched in the rains. We are sorry that we could not get firewood for him."

King Karna thought for a moment and then without any hesitation ordered his aides to chop down two beautiful wooden pillars that adorned his court. Everyone was astounded at his generosity. Without even an iota of hesitation, he had fulfilled the wishes of the villager. Such was the charitable nature of the king Karna.

Years rolled by. The king Karna lost his life in the great Mahabharata war.

Being a very charitable and generous king, he went to heaven where he had all the facilities. He was entertained by the *apsaras,* had all the comforts that he enjoyed as king while he was alive on earth and sumptuous food was always available.

But King Karna was sad. He could not eat properly; he had a loss of appetite and dyspepsia even if he ate a morsel of food. He did not know why he was suffering like this. A variety of delicacies were available in heaven, but King Karna could not enjoy it at all. That is what made him sad and melancholic.

One day, he approached Yama, the God of Death who was seated in his throne with Chithragupta, his personal assistant by his side.

"What is your problem?", asked Yama.

King Karna explained his predicament and said, "Though I have been very charitable and generous with my wealth when I was on earth, when I came here, I am not able to take my food. I have all the comforts of heaven, except that I am ill. Why is it so?".

Yama ordered his secretary, Chithragupta to go through the documents where all the good and bad deeds of persons on earth are recorded. Chithragupta accordingly checked the archives relating to King Karna. After a while, he looked up at King Karna, frowned and whispered something into Yama's ear.

Yama smiled and said, "Karna, you have been very generous with your donations when you were ruling as a king. You donated gold, silver, precious jewels, houses, cattle, firewood, and land to everyone who came to you with a request. But you forget to donate something important.

"King Karna raised his eyebrows and asked, "But what did I fail to give the needy?"

Yama replied, "You were generous and charitable in all aspects but forgot the greatest charity of all -*Annadanam.* You did not feed the poor and had forgotten to provide food to the needy, even though nobody asked you for food. That is the reason for your malady. That is your *Karma,* and it has boomeranged on you as this illness."

"What can I do about this", asked King Karna.

"The only solution for you is to go back to earth and be re-born. During that lifetime be generous with Annadanam which is the greatest gift of all. Reason is that even if you give loads of money or gold to anyone, they may still feel dissatisfied and yearn for more. But when you give food to a person, he feels satiated and blesses you as he cannot consume food beyond a limit. That is why *Annadanam* is said to be the greatest charity that anyone can do."

King Karna hung his head in shame. He realised his folly in giving everything except food to the needy because food was not very costly. He mentally prepared to go back to earth to purge his *Karma*.

Moral: Annadanam, giving food to the needy is the greatest of all charities.

Annadanam: Providing food to the hungry and needy.

Mahabharata War: A great war fought between the Pandavas and Kauravas. (Ref. *Mahabharata epic*)

Apsaras: Dancers in heaven who entertain the residents there.

Chitragupta: Personal Assistant to Yama, the God of Death who archives the good and bad deeds of man.

Karma: Actions of a person and the results arising from them.

28. The Lost Opportunity.

I was sitting on the patio in the morning reading a novel by Agatha Christie. The sky was cloudy the sun had risen from the east. There was a slight drizzle. Suddenly in front of me in the overcast sky, there appeared a beautiful rainbow resplendent in the seven colours – a perfect rainbow. I called out to Jaya and Vijaya to come out immediately to see this beautiful celestial spectacle.

"Quick, kids," I shouted, "Come at once, you will miss this spectacle if you come late."

Both the kids came running and looked at the perfect rainbow with wonder. Jaya ran and fetched her mobile phone to click pictures of it.

"Why did you ask us to hurry, Thathu? It could have waited."

"No, kids, celestial spectacles will not wait for anyone. You have to see them while they last, or it will be like the shepherd who lost the opportunity to enter El Dorado"

"Thathu", pleaded the kids, "Tell us the story of the Shepherd", and I told them the story of the Lost Opportunity…

· · · · · · · · · · · ·

Once upon a time there was a shepherd boy who used to go to the mountains in the foothills of the Himalayas. Every morning he used to take his sheep to graze in the fields in the valley adjoining the Himalayas.

Once this boy chanced to see a monk seated on a rock meditating and he stood nearby and watched him. The monk had his eyes closed and was taking slow, deep breaths. The shepherd concluded that the monk was meditating. He stood at a distance in reverence with folded hands watching the monk.

After a while the monk opened his eyes and his eyes fell on the shepherd who was standing nearby and beckoned him to come near him.

"Who are you and what are you doing here", asked the monk.

"I am a shepherd grazing my sheep in the field there. I came to you when I saw you meditating."

"Son", said the monk, "I am hungry and thirsty. Can you provide me with something to eat and drink?"

"Sure, I shall bring you some bread and milk.", said the boy and ran to the shade of a tree where he had kept his satchel and came back with a loaf of bread and a glassful of milk.

The monk was satisfied and ate the bread and drank the milk. "Thank you, my son,", he said. "You have been kind to me, I will show you a wonderful sight if you come with me".

The monk led the way and the shepherd followed. Soon they reached a crevice on a rockface near the mountain. The monk stood in front of the crevice and looked up at the sun. the sun was almost straight above their heads and sunlight was slowly falling on to the crevice creeping like a glimmering light.

The monk and the shepherd stood gazing at the crevice. Exactly as the sun's rays fell on the gap in the crevice, there was a thunderous sound and the crevice seemed to split open. The shepherd and the monk stood aghast in wonder at the spectacle that was unfolding before them.

Through the gap in the crevice, they could see a beautiful valley beyond. It was resplendent with flowering plants and trees. There were small ponds and gurgling rivulets which were producing a musical sound. The trees abounded with fruits, and birds were singing from the treetops. The valley looked warm and inviting despite the cold outside where the monk and the shepherd stood.

"This my son is Shangri La. This crevice opens to reveal it only once in one thousand years on a particular day and particular time when the sun shines from the heaven directly above our heads. I had been meditating and waiting for this moment here as I am going to cross over from here and go to the opposite side. Life there is like heaven on earth, you must experience it to believe it. I am now going to cross over to the other side. Once you cross, you cannot come back to this earth."

The shepherd boy was listening to all this in wonder. He just could not believe his eyes that such a heaven on earth has opened before him.

The saint accosted him, "If you are willing to come with me, I will take you to Shangri La. You will find eternal happiness there. Want to come with me?"

The boy thought for a moment. "If I go alone, it will be an act of selfishness. Why not I run to my village and get my parents, brothers, and sisters to accompany me to Shangri La." He told the monk. I will run to my village and bring my family quickly and all of us will cross to the other side immediately.

The monk warned him, "My son, the portal to this heaven will be open only for a short while. Unless you hurry, you won't be able to cross over. Come with me, do not tarry. If you don't cross now, you may lose this golden opportunity. An important opportunity like this does not knock twice."

"No, master", I cannot cross alone. I will get my family members also.

The monk bid goodbye to the lad and crossed over. There was a flash of light and the monk disappeared.

The shepherd ran down the hill to his family. Panting, he explained all of what happened and the whole family ran together to the crevice to enter El dorado.

But alas, when they reached there, they found that the portal had closed, and the rocky crevice was all that was seen.

The boy and his family returned home in despair. The monk was never again seen in the valley.

Moral: Opportunity does not knock twice.

Shangri La: A remote beautiful imaginary place where life approaches perfection: Utopia.

29. The Donkey and the Jackal

"Thathu", asked Jaya as soon as she returned from school, "Which is the tallest mountain in the world?"

"Why, the Mount Everest of course", I said without any hesitation, for that was one thing I was sure about. "It is 8849 meters or 29,031 feet in height. But why do you ask?", I queried.

"No, Thathu, I had an argument with a girl in my class. She said that the mountain Mauna Kea in Hawaii is the tallest. She was adamant about it."

"Well," I said, "In a way both of you are correct. But the Mount Everest is the tallest when measured from the sea level and that is how the height of a mountain is calculated. Mauna Kea is an inactive volcano in Hawaii in the Pacific Ocean, half of which is submerged in the ocean. So, from base to its summit, it will be the tallest, but not from sea level."

"But don't go arguing with anyone about such things as you are wasting your time, like the jackal which argued with a donkey."

That triggered off a spate of requests, not only from the kids but also from Amma and Appa, "Hey, I have not heard that story, tell us."

And I began recounting the story of the Donkey and the Jackal…

....

Once upon a time in a forest there lived a jackal and a donkey. They were not friends because the donkey was afraid of the jackal and the jackal was always arguing with the donkey. The lion was the king of the jungle and all the animals in the forest followed the advice and suggestions of the king.

One day, after the rainy season was over the donkey was grazing in a green grassy field when the jackal approached it and asked, "What are you eating my friend?"

There is so much of purple grass here and I am feeding myself on the grass growing here.

The jackal was surprised. "Purple grass? Did you say 'purple' grass?"

The donkey looked perplexed. "Why, yes the grass all over the field is purple. Can't you see?"

The jackal snickered, "Purple? Ha, ha you are foolish, the grass is green, can't you see? Everywhere the grass is green, not purple."

"What?", shouted the donkey, this is purple in colour. You are colour blind and cannot detect it."

"You stupid ass", said the jackal, "Grass is always green and not purple."

"Can you not see the purple grass spread all over the field", retorted the donkey. "You must be a fool to say that the grass is green. It is not".

Ultimately, the argument went on for some time and both were angry, not giving in to the other's opinion. They hence decided to go to the king and get justice.

The Donkey and the Jackal went to the king. The king of the forest was the lion which was seated on a big rock amid a clearing in the jungle. Both bowed low and the Jackal spoke up, "Your majesty, there is dispute between us, and I want your esteemed self to sort it out for us and mete out justice.

"What is your problem?", roared the king. I will sort it out now itself.

The Donkey and the Jackal explained their respective points of view regarding the colour of the grass in the field. Both claimed that they were right and the other, wrong.

The lion looked at both gave a loud roar and said, "I hereby order that the Jackal be sentenced to one month in prison. The donkey being innocent is free to go."

The donkey trotted away braying happily.

The Jackal stood there dismayed over the judgement of the king. He felt that the king was unjust and partial to the donkey. The Jackal addressed the king, "Your majesty, I have a doubt to clear. What is your opinion, is the grass green or purple?"

"Definitely", replied the lion, "Grass is always green, not purple".

This surprised the Jackal. "Then why your majesty, you let the Donkey go and punished poor me?", asked the Jackal dismally.

"The lion gave another big roar and said, "Of course, the Donkey is wrong. Grass cannot be purple. But after all it is a silly donkey, and its nature is to be foolish. But you are a wise jackal, and you should not have argued with a donkey and wasted your time and my time over such a silly matter. If you were convinced that the grass is green, you shouldn't have argued with the stupid donkey. That is why I punished you. Don't behave like this hereafter."

"Be careful in life", continued the Lion. "There are stupid animals all around you. Wisdom lies in avoiding arguments with such silly animals like donkeys and wasting your time. You are at fault, really."

The Jackal hung its head in shame.

Moral: Don't argue with foolish people wasting your time. Avoid arguments when stupid folk try to argue with you over silly matters.

30. The Benefit of Co-operation

Both the children were quarrelling. Hearing the commotion, I went upstairs to their study to see what the matter was.

"Thathu", complained Jaya, "Vijaya wants my crayons to do her drawing homework while I too need it to complete my assignment. She is being adamant".

"Why Vijaya", I tried to intercede, "Why don't you do your maths assignment while Jaya completes hers using the crayons and then you can finish your drawing assignment using her crayons. What happened to your box of crayons?", I asked her.

"Thathu, I forgot to bring it from school. I left it on my desk when I came home on Friday", she replied sheepishly.

"Doesn't matter", I pacified her, "You can get it back on Monday. You girls should learn to co-operate between yourselves just like the Pandavas did when Bhishma gave them a test."

Their immediate differences forgotten, the kids echoed in unison, "Thathu, tell us that story." And I told them the story of the Benefit of Co-operation…

. . . .

The Pandavas and Kauravas were always quarrelling among themselves. The Pandavas were five in number and the Kauravas were a hundred. Right from childhood there was animosity between both the groups. Even as children, the Kauravas troubled and molested the Pandavas whenever they got a chance. There was always bad blood between them.

One day, the grand sire of the family, Bhishma called them and said, "Children, you are always quarrelling among yourselves. I am going to give you a test and want to see who wins. I will serve your meals in two different halls today and give you only half an hour to finish your meals and report back to me".

"But what is the test?", asked Yudhishtra, the eldest of the Pandavas and Duryodhana, the eldest of the Kauravas."

"I will tell you", said Bhishma, "I will tie two long sticks to your arms so that you cannot bend your elbow. I will then serve you the meals. All of you should finish eating in half an hour but you should not untie the sticks that have been tied to your arms."

"But how can I eat without bending my elbow?", asked Duryodhana. This is a foolish test."

Yudhishtra kept quiet and did not respond.

Bhishma took them to two different halls and the guards, splinted their arms with bamboo sticks. Then the children were supplied with delicious food on the table in plates with bowls and spoons, but they could not bend their elbows to eat the food. The guards left the hall and Bhishma stood guard checking that no foul play occurred.

Bhishma first went to the hall where the Kauravas were served food. Duryodhana and others were sitting perplexed as to what to do. Duryodhana bent forward and tried to eat the food from the plate as animals do but ended up smearing his face with curry and curds. Everyone tried to do the same.

Bhishma left the room and went to the adjoining room where the Pandavas were served food. To his utter surprise, he found that they had almost finished their meal. As they could not bend their elbows, with a straight arm each one was feeding the other and thus had finished their meal.

Bhishma called the Pandavas and Kauravas to his side and told them. "Look here, Duryodhana, the Pandavas finished their meal in no time as there was co-operation among them. But you and your brothers never thought of co-operating like this and are still quarrelling with the Pandavas frequently."

Bhishma continued, "No man is an island. We all need help from others at various times and for various reasons. Wisdom lies in co-operating with others and making the best of life. This is the lesson that I wanted to teach you through this simple test. Now go forth and play among yourselves without malice".

Duryodhana left the room moping.

Moral: One should always co-operate with others and not quarrel for silly reasons. No man is an island. In life we will have to seek help from others and give help to others who need it.

31. The Clever Crow.

Thathu, Thathu", called out Jaya when she returned from school, "I lent my fountain pen to a friend in my class, and she forgot to return it. She probably went home putting it in her pocket. I have to do my homework and my class teacher insists that we should do our cursive writing homework using the fountain pen only as ball point pens spoil our handwriting."

"True", said I, "Using the fountain pen improves your handwriting and ballpoint pens do not do that. For today, I will lend you my pen. I'll give you a suggestion on how not to lose your fountain pen when you lend it to someone,", I told her.

"How is that possible, Thathu?", asked both together.

"Keep the cap of the pen with you and give them only the pen to write with. They cannot put the pen in their pocket by mistake if they don't have the cap with them. This way, you will not lose your pen. You should be like the clever crow which played a trick on the fox", I concluded.

"Oh, Thathu, tell us that story", begged the children and I told them the story of the Clever Crow…

. . . .

Once upon a time in a village, there was an old woman who lived alone in a hut. She had no children to look after her and spent her time cooking and making snacks which she sold to the travellers who passed by her house. She used to make very tasty *Vadas*. She used to sit in the veranda in front of her house and make the *Vadas* frying them in a pan of oil. Her *Vadas* were very tasty and was sought after by all the folk in the village.

After frying the first batch of *Vadas* for the day, she used to give one Vada to a crow which had made its abode in a tree near her hut. The crow had built a nest on the branches of the tree and had laid eggs there. The eggs had hatched into nestlings which were taken care of by the crow feeding them and giving them bits of the food that it scavenged from various places. Soon these little nestlings grew into bigger birds and a day came when they flew away from the nest, never to return. The crow who had grown old, was left alone in the tree.

The old woman had seen all that had happened and felt a kinship with the bird. It was because of this affinity for the bird that she gave a *Vada* to it every day.

One day, as usual, the woman gave the crow a *Vada* and a fox from a nearby jungle was passing by the tree. The crow flew on to a low branch of the tree with the *Vada* held in its beak. The aroma of the fried Vada reached the nostrils of the fox. Its mouth started watering and the fox wanted to get the Vada that the crow was eating. Slowly, the cunning fox came and sat at the foot of the tree and looking up and started conversing with the crow.

"Oh, beautiful bird", the fox said, "You are so smart and graceful. You look much better than all those birds I see in the jungle. You look stately and strong. I am sure that your voice also must be as sweet as yourself. I am sure that you sing better and sweeter than the cuckoo or the nightingale. Pray, sing me a song so that I can return to the jungle with your sweet voice ringing in my ears".

The crow felt flattered by the praise showered on it and thought that it should sing a song for the fox. It opened its mouth and sang, "Caw, Caw, Caw". No sooner had the crow opened its mouth, than the *Vada* fell straight down at the feet of the fox and the fox snatched it and ran away into the jungle. The crow felt outwitted by the cunning fox and was helpless.

Days passed by. One morning, as usual the old woman gave a *Vada* to the crow and the crow flew to the treetop with it. As soon as the crow sat on the branch of the tree, the fox appeared below and sat there. The fox thought that this was a different crow. But the crow had become clever after the last lesson. "Once bitten, twice shy", the crow thought. Slowly the fox started as usual talking and praising the crow and its beauty. The crow sat silently with the *Vada* in its mouth smiling to itself.

At last, the fox beseeched the crow to sing a song. The crow very carefully placed the *Vada* in a small cleft in the tree, flew down to a branch lower than where it was sitting and with its beak pecked at a beehive that was in the branch and flew away. The branch broke and the beehive fell on the fox's head. The bees started stinging the fox all over. "Ow, ow", cried the fox and started dancing around with pain. Yelping loudly in pain, it ran into the jungle never to be seen near the tree again.

The crow went back to its perch and ate the *Vada* which it had carefully stowed away.

The woman watching this drama from the veranda of her hut was cackling with joy. "It serves the fox right for trying to outwit you. You learnt a lesson last time and now that has made you clever." Saying this, the old woman gave another *Vada* to the crow.

Moral: In life don't be duped by the same trick twice. Once bitten twice shy.

Vada: A savoury fried snack from South India made of ground lentils.

32. The Emperor and the Sage.

Vijaya was eating a bowl of walnuts. "Where did you get them from?", asked Jaya.

"I begged Amma to give me walnuts as I was feeling hungry", was Vijaya's reply.

"Give me some from your bowl", asked Jaya,

"No, I want this for myself. I got it from Amma, if you want go and ask her", was her curt reply.

I was listening to this tête-à-tête with interest. "Girls, have you heard of the story of the sage who refused to accept alms from the emperor? Come I will tell you the story. But before that, Vijaya, I want you to share the walnuts with your sister".

Promptly, Vijaya gave Jaya half the walnuts in the bowl, and I started recounting the story of the Emperor and the Sage…

. . . .

Once upon a time a part of North India was ruled by a Moghul Emperor. Delhi was his capital. He was said to be very philanthropic and generous to his subjects and anyone who came to his court seeking alms or justice was never turned back empty-handed. He was also very pious and prayed five times a day.

The king lived in a palace with his queen and his young son who would become king later. The palace was large and sprawling with beautiful gardens on all four sides.

One day a sage came to the court of the king. He was a sage who had wandered down from the Himalayas and was visiting all the sacred shrines in India. He had come to Delhi to seek help from the emperor in the form of alms for his travel.

The sage entered the court of the emperor. All the ministers and courtiers were present, but the emperor was not on the throne. The chief minister informed the sage that the emperor was inside the prayer room praying to God.

The sage seemed surprised. "Oh, the emperor is praying?", he queried. "Then don't disturb him". The sage turned to leave the court. The chief minister immediately ran to him and implored, "Oh, honourable *swamiji*, do not go away. Please wait for some more time, the emperor will join us shortly." The minister offered the sage a seat and the sage sat down.

Shortly, the emperor walked into the court, and everyone stood up. The sage also stood up. The emperor, seeing the sage, immediately came up to him and offered his salutations. "Welcome, *Swamiji*", the emperor said, "I am sorry to have kept you waiting, I was praying to God Almighty"

The sage smiled and asked, "What were you praying for, *Jahan Panaah?*"

The emperor raised his palms to heavens and looked up. I was praying for prosperity, health, and welfare of all my subjects, my family and myself. I asked God to give me the strength and blessings to expand my empire."

The sage raised his brows, "You entreated God to give you all this?", he asked, with surprise in his voice.

The emperor nodded in acquiescence. "Yes, I asked God to give me all these as that will increase the prosperity and wealth of my kingdom and subjects."

The sage replied to the emperor with folded hands, "Oh, J*ahan Panaah*, I came seeking alms from you. But I found that you were begging alms from God himself. How can I take alms from someone who himself is a beggar?"

Without another word, the sage left the court and continued his journey. The emperor and the whole court stood stunned and speechless.

Moral: Do not pray to God for material riches. It makes you no different from a beggar.

Swamiji: A Hindu religious leader.

Jahan Panaah: King, Emperor, Your majesty. (In Hindi)

33. Why Crows tilt their heads while looking.

My daughter along with Jaya and Vijaya had come from the U.S to spend their summer holidays with us for a month. The children being born and brought up in the U.S were getting accustomed to the climate in India and the customs and traditions here. I had taken them to the nearby temple of Sri Krishna in the morning while my wife and daughter were cooking lunch.

After the preparation was over, my wife put a ladleful of cooked rice on a small dish that was placed in the courtyard at the back of the house.

"Why are you doing this Ammamma?", asked the kids. For they called her 'Ammamma', meaning grandmother in Tamil and Malayalam.

Our ancestors sometimes visit us in the form of crows to see how we are living, whether we are following our culture and whether we are honest, truthful, and good. So, I place food for the crows every morning after I cook our lunch to feed our ancestors before we partake of our lunch. It is a tradition from time immemorial."

The kids were sitting on the sill waiting for the crows to come and feed on the cooked rice. Soon a loud cawing was heard, and a murder of crows appeared as if from nowhere and summoned their kith and kin to partake in the food that was served by Ammamma.

"Thathu, why is that crow looking at me tilting its head as if it has a squint?" observed Jaya.

"Well, well, kids, come on, it is time now for the story of why the crow tilts its head while looking", said I.

The kids ran to my side, and I began telling the story why the Crows tilt their heads while looking…

....

Rama, Sita and Lakshmana went to the forest as requested by their father, Dasaratha. In the forest, Lakshmana built a beautiful cottage with bamboo, clay and thatched it with large palm leaves, a technique that he had learnt during his *Gurukul* training. There was a clearing in the forest with beautiful flowering plants and fruit bearing trees all around. It was called Chitrakoota.

One day, after lunch, Rama and Sita were sitting under a nearby tree chatting and Lakshmana was busy getting things ready to go hunting.

A wicked demon named Kakasura, in the guise of a crow, came near the cottage. (Kaka = crow, in Sanskrit). After chatting for some time, Rama lay down to rest with his head on Sita's lap. Gradually he fell into a slumber and Sita was sitting with her eyes closed and her lips murmuring a prayer.

Kakasura thought that this was the apt time to attack Sita and flew low and hopped near Sita's feet. Then it started pecking at Sita's feet. Fearing that she would awaken Ram, Sita clenched her teeth and kept quiet without making any sound even though the pain was unbearable, and blood was flowing out of the wound. She tried to throw stones at the crow, but it came back repeatedly to peck at her feet.

Suddenly, Rama opened his eyes and saw the scene in front of him and realised immediately who the demon was. He plucked a long blade of grass from nearby and recited a *mantra*. The blade of grass turned into a sharp and powerful arrow, which Rama flung it at the crow. The arrow chased the crow which tried to escape, but wherever the crow flew, the arrow followed. Finally, the crow understood that it had no way to escape and came back and fell at the feet of Rama, seeking forgiveness.

"Once I have shot an arrow, there is no way for me to take it back and it has to find a target. Furthermore, you need to be punished for your senseless act of pecking at Sita's feet. Hence, I'll order the arrow to target your right eye only and spare your life. The crow bowed before him. The arrow struck the crow's eye and blinded him in one eye. Kakasura left the place with a chastened mind.

From that day, it is said that crows always tilt their heads to one side when looking at anything with one eye.

Moral: In Indian culture, it is important to feed the birds and animals and there is often a story connected to this to encourage people to do so.

Sri Krishna: One of the avatars of Lord Vishnu.

Rama, Sita, Lakshmana: They are characters in the epic *Ramayana.*

Gurukul: A gurukul is a traditional school in India with students living near their guru (teacher), often in the same dwelling, as a sort of family.

Mantra: A short chant repeated during meditation or prayers.

34. Satyavan and Savithri

While in India with us for the vacation, the kids one day came running to me, "Thathu, Ammamma says that she is fasting and has not eaten any food since morning. She said that she will eat food only after the sun sets and the lamp is lit in front of the altar where we have our pooja. Why is that so?"

*"Ah", I said, "Today is an auspicious day when Ammamma observes a **Vratham**. She will eat only at sundown after lighting the lamp and offering pooja. There is a story connected with this, and I will tell you the story if you come and sit beside me."*

And thus, I began telling them the story of Satyavan and Savithri…

. . . .

Once upon a time there was a king in a kingdom in the north of India. He ruled his subjects well. There were enough food grains in the kingdom and enough rains leading to a bounty harvest year after year. The king was a very pious and kind man and was benevolent towards his subjects. There was nothing wanting for him except one worry. He had no children, and he was getting old. That was his major anguish. He had conducted many *Yagas,* but despite this, he was childless.

Once a sage came to his palace and told him. "Oh, mighty king", he said, "You will be blessed with a daughter very soon if you pray to the goddess *Gayathri.* The king followed his advice and prayed daily to the goddess. He also undertook strict austerities to propitiate the goddess.

True to the sage's blessing, the queen gave birth to a beautiful little princess and named her Savithri, a synonym of the name *Gayathri.*

The child grew up to be a beautiful young girl of eighteen, when the king sought suitors for his daughter. But no prince wooed her or was ready to marry her. Years rolled by. One day, the king called his daughter Savithri to his side and said, "Look here, my girl you are grown up and already passed the age of being married. But I have failed to find a suitable groom for you. I wish that you go into the world there and find for yourself a suitable husband."

Savithri set out from the kingdom accompanied by few of her companions and a few guards and went in search of an appropriate groom for herself.

Far away in another kingdom ruled a king named Dyumatsena. He had a young son by the name of Satyavan. Satyavan was a very handsome youth of twenty-one and had striking features and a muscular body.

Once an enemy king attacked the kingdom and drove the king, the queen and Satyavan away from the kingdom and usurped his kingdom. In the fight for the kingdom Dyumatsena had been rendered blind.

Having no other way all three of them made their way into the forest and lived there in a cottage with the help of some hermits who were staying nearby. Satyavan used to go into the forest daily and collect firewood and hunt for small animals and gather fruits and tubers which he would bring home for dinner. His mother, the queen used to cook food for them. They were leading a very frugal life.

Despite being banished from the kingdom, Satyavan did not lose hope. He worked hard from dawn to dusk hunting, chopping wood, and cultivating fruits and vegetables around the cottage. These physical efforts made him more handsome and his body, more strapping. He turned out to be an Adonis.

It was into this forest that Savithri and her maids chanced to come. Feeling thirsty, they approached the cottage of Satyavan and Savithri entered it. Satyavan had gone out for cutting wood. Savithri saw the old blind king and the queen there. They welcomed her and offered the princess and her companions food and water. After resting awhile, the king and the queen introduced themselves to her.

After thanking them, Savithri came out of the cottage to join her entourage, when she noticed a sinewy, extremely handsome youth walking towards the cottage.

Satyavan's mother introduced the young man to Savithri as her son. One look at him made Savithri decide as to who would be her future husband. It was love at first sight. Satyavan also fell in love with her instantly.

The group left the cottage and went back to the kingdom.

The next day, Savithri went to meet her parents. "Father," she said bowing to her father, "I have found my life partner". On hearing this the king was overjoyed.

He asked her the details of what had transpired the previous day. Savithri explained in detail all the events that occurred and who the blind king was. Knowing that Satyavan was a prince, the king was delighted. He ordered all arrangements to be made to go to the forest and meet Satyavan's parents. He also ordered arrangements to be made for the marriage.

It was then that Sage Narada walked into the court. The king and queen welcomed him and seated him. Savithri bowed before him to seek his blessings. He blessed her with the words, "**Deerga Sumangali Bhava**"- (May you live with your husband for a long time).

Savithri's father was overjoyed at this good news that his daughter had told him. He took the visit of sage Narada as a good omen. The king informed Sage Narada about the imminent marriage between Savithri and Satyavan. He also told him about Satyavan's parents.

Hearing this Sage Narada frowned, "Satyavan?", he asked with a tremulous voice, "It is better if Savithri does not wed Satyavan."

"But why", asked the king. His parents are king and queen even though they have lost their kingdom and Satyavan is a very capable and handsome prince."

"No, still it is not right", said Sage Narada. "I would advise you to renege on this decision."

The king wanted to know why, and Sage Narada explained, "Exactly one year from today Satyavan will die. His life ends then. This is fate and cannot be prevented or changed by any of us."

Savithri, who had been silent till now spoke up. "My salutations to you sage, but I cannot change my mind once I have resolved that Satyavan will be my husband. There is no going back on that decision. That is final". She was adamant.

The king was at a loss for words. Sage Narada said, "I am leaving now. But I am pleased with your resolute decision. Let good luck come to you. My blessing to you shall come true."

Soon Satyavan and Savithri were married and Savithri, as is the Indian custom went to live in the forest with her husband and his parents. She adjusted to that life in no time like fish to water.

Weeks and months rolled by. At last, the fateful day arrived when Satyavan would breathe his last. Savithri had been observing strict penance for the three days preceding this and woke up early in the morning and had her bath and prayers. She said that she would accompany Satyavan to the forest where he went to cut wood. Satyavan and her father-in-law tried their best to dissuade her from going. But Savithri was adamant.

"I want to come with you only today, my dear," she told Satyavan, "I have never asked you before and never will ask hereafter." She also managed to convince his parents to let her go.

Satyavan and Savithri went deep into the forest and Satyavan proceeded to cut wood and chop it into pieces and bundle it. By noon, he was exhausted, and he and Savithri partook of the curd rice which she had brought from home. Satyavan said that he was tired and wanted to rest awhile. He lay down under the shade of a tree with his head on Savithri's lap. He drifted off to sleep. Savithri continued to pray.

Suddenly, there was a flash of light in front of her and she saw a divine form standing before her. It was Yamaraj, the God of Death. He had come to claim Satyavan's life.

"Oh, noble Yamaraj", Savithri addressed him, "I know you have come for the life of my husband. I beseech you to spare his life. We have been married for one year only and have not lived life fully".

"Impossible", replied Yamaraj, "Satyavan's life ends today and there is no option for him but to return to the land of the dead. I have to take him." With these words, Yamaraj, tied up Satyavan's life in his lariat and dragged the soul out of the lifeless body of Satyavan. Yamaraj, began his journey walking south.

Savithri, with folded hands, followed behind him. She entreated Yamaraj to spare her husband's life and requested him to return his soul to his body. She quoted from the scriptures and praised him for the righteous way in which he meted out justice to the dead souls.

After a while, Yamaraj paused looked back and said, "Savithri, I am touched by your devotion to your husband. Ask what boon you want, except the life of your husband".

Oh, noble Yamaraj", Savithri requested, "My father-in-law who is blind must gain back his vision and his original strength and valour".

"So be it", blessed the God of Death and continued his way.

But Savithri did not give up. She continued to follow him praising righteousness, rectitude, and other qualities of the God of Death.

After a while, the Yamaraj paused and asked Savithri, "I will give you one more boon, apart from the life of your husband".

"My father-in-law should regain all his lost kingdom and wealth and be restored to the throne as the king".

"So be it", blessed Yamaraj.

Still, Savithri followed him deep into the forest towards the south speaking to him, praising him and entreating him to spare her husband's life.

At last, Yamaraj turned back to her and said, "I am greatly satisfied with your devotion to your father-in-law. You may ask any other boon you would want, except the life of your husband".

"My father-in-law has only one son, Satyavan. Please bless him with many more children", Savithri pleaded.

So be it", the God of Death said, your father-in-law shall have many children.

And he proceeded to go south with Satyavan's soul.

Savithri did not give up. Her doggedness was boundless. She continued behind Yamaraj.

Yamaraj seemed irritated. "Now what is it you want, except your husband's life", he asked. I have given you enough boons so far. "Alright, I shall permit one more last boon for you. What do you want to ask?"

"Just like my father-in-law, I too should be blessed with many children", she said bowing to him.

"So be it", Yamaraj replied, "You will have many children".

Yamaraj had answered without thinking. No sooner had he said the words, than he realized his mistake. He could not revoke a boon which he himself had given.

"So, honourable Yamaraj", Savithri said bowing to him and folding her hands in prayer, "You know that to have many children, my husband should be alive. Hence it is your duty to restore my husband back to life to make your words come true".

Yamaraj was taken aback by her wit and wisdom. He laughed aloud, "For the first time, Savithri, you have defeated me with your words. I am pleased with your unflinching devotion to your husband, and I hereby release your husband's soul. He shall live for a hundred years. Savithri thanked him and returned to where her husband's body lay. Within a matter of minutes, Satyavan woke up as if from sleep and asked her. "What happened? I had a strange dream as if some god came near me and carried me away to a far-off land. But now on awakening, I understand that it was but a dream. Savithri smiled hugged her husband and said nothing.

They returned to their cottage where their parents were excitedly waiting for them. Her father-in-law had fully recovered, and his eyesight had returned. Soon a messenger came from the royal court of his kingdom to say that the tyrant king who had defeated him had been killed in a revolt by the people and now the kingdom had no king. They wanted him to come and take up the reins again.

They all returned to the kingdom and lived happily ever after.

Moral: Persistence and wits pays. Devotion and attachment to one's husband is the duty of every Indian woman.

Gayathri: A Hindu goddess

Vratham: Means vow or resolution and refers to pious observances such as fasting and pilgrimage.

Yaga: Sacrifice, Devotion, Offering. (To the Gods)

Narada: A celestial sage, who travels all the worlds and foretells the future occasionally.

Yamaraj: The god of Death in Hindu Mythology.

35. The Banyan seed and the Jack Fruit

*Jaya and Vijaya joined me when I went to the temple on a Sunday morning. As we were circumambulating the sanctum sanctorum, Jaya observed the sprawling banyan tree at the back of the temple. It was giving a cool shade and was populated with a variety of birds. Devotees were sitting in its cool shade partaking of the **Prasad** which had been offered in the temple to all the devotees.*

Vijaya picked up the small seed of the tree which had fallen at the foot of the tree and remarked, "What a small seed for such a large tree!".

"Well, children, I'll tell you an interesting story about the Banyan seed when we are returning home after our prayers." And on our return, I told them the story of the Banyan seed and the Jack Fruit…

. . . .

Once, a traveller was walking through a thickly wooded jungle. He was exhausted and felt very thirsty. He saw a small pool of crystal-clear water near a banyan tree. He had some snacks in a bundle that his wife had provided and ate the snacks and drank water to his heart's content. As he felt tired, he sat at the base of the banyan tree and soon felt drowsy. He started thinking of God's mysterious ways.

"How great is God for providing for man and animals alike", he thought, "This large and sprawling banyan tree beside this cool clear-water pool is an ideal resting place for travellers. The tree is also held sacred by the Hindus of India. Also, it serves as a watering hole for animals and birds. They can quench their thirst and rest awhile. The abundant foliage of the tree provides cool, comfortable shade to all".

Thinking thus, he looked up. On most of the branches, he found bunches of figs, very small in size, on which birds were feeding. "How foolish God is he muttered to himself. Such a huge tree with such ramification of branches and roots has such a small fruit and seed!", he exclaimed.

"Look at the jack fruit tree", he exclaimed to himself. "It is also a large tree but with large, delicious fruits edible to man, birds and animals. The fig of this tree is no use to man at all".

Just then a banyan fig fell on his forehead. He rubbed the area as it was mildly painful.

Suddenly he realised what a fool he had been. He had blamed God for creating the small and tiny banyan fig with tiny seeds. Indeed, if a jack fruit had fallen on his head, what would have been his fate!

The man smiled to himself and said a prayer. Indeed, strange are the ways of God. The banyan tree is created to give shade to man and animals and provide a haven for birds. Hence, its fruit and seed are small and tiny so as not to harm anyone on which it falls.

"God is great", he mumbled to himself, "I am a fool to have misunderstood Nature and creation".

Moral: Everything in Nature is created with a specific purpose and with a specific need. True, the razor blade is sharp, but cannot cut a tree, an axe can cut a tree, but can't be used for shaving. Everything has its own uses and is helpful in different ways.

Sanctum Sanctorum: The innermost holy place in a temple where the idol of the God is kept.

Prasad: A offering of food made to God and later shared by the devotees.

36. Truth Will Out.

Why are you late from school?", Amma asked Jaya when she came half an hour late.

"I had a special class today after the usual classes", she said, avoiding Amma's eyes.

I knew she was not speaking the truth.

"She stayed back to eat an ice cream from the tuck-shop in school", Vijaya let the cat out of the bag.

With a sheepish smile, Jaya acquiesced.

"Don't lie to anybody, especially to your parents. Don't you guys know the story of the four students who lied to their principal?", I asked.

"Thathu, tell us that story shouted both together", and I ended up telling the story how Truth will Out...

• • • • • • • • • • • • •

There were four friends in a college. They were all very close to each other and always partook of college activities together. They also went frequently out of station on picnics. One friend's father owned a car which he used to lend to his son to go on trips to nearby places.

Once the friends decided to go to Ooty which was a very beautiful hill station in south India. It is popularly called the Queen of the Western Ghats. It was the summer capital of the British when they ruled India. Ooty is attractive to the tourists because of its pleasant climate and its beautiful parks and lakes.

There is a flower show in Ooty during the month of May every year. It attracts many tourists from India and abroad. It was to attend this flower show that the four friends decided to go on a Friday afternoon shirking the afternoon lectures. Little did they know that the Professor 'Sour-face' who taught the classes that afternoon had announced a short test on the following Monday morning.

The four drove the car to Ooty and spent the weekend in Ooty visiting the flower show and enjoying a break from the dreary 'lectures' of Professor 'Sour-face'. They enjoyed two days of fun and frolic. After spending two days there, they drove back to their college early morning on Monday. But by the time they reached their classes, the professor had already started the test and hence they were not allowed to enter the examination hall. Their delay in arrival at the examination hall was reported to the principal, whom they called 'Smiley-face'.

The principal summoned all the four friends to the office. He smiled at them and said, "So, boys did you enjoy your weekend at Ooty?"

"Yes Sir", they replied sheepishly.

"Didn't you know that there is a test to be held this morning?"

"No Sir, we did not know as we were absent from class when the announcement was made on Friday. This morning, we started very early from Ooty, but our car's tyre had a puncture on the way, and we were delayed because of the flat tyre", said the student who was the owner of the car. All the four nodded vigorously and chorused. "Yes Sir, if there was no flat tyre, we would have reached in time for the test"

"That was a grievous mistake on your part", said the principal. "Not knowing about the examination and coming to the college late on a Monday morning is an unpardonable misdemeanour. I cannot pardon that. What shall I do with the four of you?", the principal asked himself.

"Excuse us this time, Sir, we will never repeat such a mistake again", pleaded all four.

"Okay then", the principal continued, smiling, "I will do one thing. I will give you a very short test and if you answer correctly, I will give you full marks for the test. If not all of you will get zero."

The students had no other way except to nod their heads in assent.

The principal seated each one of them in the four corners of a large hall. He took their mobile phones and placed them on his desk and gave them each a sheet of paper and told them, "You have only five minutes to answer the two questions which I shall dictate. After five minutes, I will take your answer sheets and evaluate them. Till that I will be here in this room itself and you shall not discuss among yourselves."

The students sat in the rooms expectantly. The questions he asked were.

1. Which tyre of your car had a flat?
2. The name of the town or village where this occurred.

The students knew that they were at a loss as to what to write. For their car never had a flat tyre. They had lied. They were late because they had risen very late from bed after a night of revelry. All four of them wrote what came to their mind – lies – knowing fully well that they were bluffing.

The principal stood there with a triumphant smile and declared, "Boys, I know that you were fibbing, so I decided to defeat you with the same lies. All four of you are suspended from college for the next two days".

The four of them stood dumbfounded unable to respond.

> **Moral:**   Truth will out despite all efforts to conceal it. Truth always comes out.

37. How the Squirrel got its lines

'Squeak, squeak' went the squirrel sitting on the branch of the mango tree, flipping its tail with each sound. The kids Jaya and Vijaya who had come to India to enjoy the summer vacation were standing at the bedroom window watching the squirrel squeaking and flipping its tail as it nibbled at a ripe mango.

"Thathu, why is the squirrel having three white lines on its back?", asked Vijaya observing the squirrel sitting on its haunch.

"Oh, that", I remarked. "I will tell you a story of How the Squirrel got its Lines…

. . . .

When Ravana, the evil king of Sri Lanka kidnapped Lord Rama's wife, Sita, Lord Rama along with his brother Lakshmana and an army of monkeys and bears reached the southernmost point of India to cross over to Sri Lanka. Seeing the mighty ocean in front of them, they stood dismayed. "How can we cross this mighty ocean?", they thought. "We are so many and have to cross over to Sri Lanka. We have no boats or ships with us."

Lord Rama came up with a solution. He said, "I will do penance for three days to propitiate the Varuna, God of the oceans. He will grant my wish to part the ocean and give way to me". Saying thus, Lord Rama sat down on the seashore in deep meditation for three days and three nights with neither food nor sleep".

But alas! At the end of three days, nothing happened. Lord Varuna did not condescend to answer Lord Rama's prayers. Enraged, Lord Rama got up from his meditation and took up arms. He aimed an arrow at the ocean and declared, "Oh, Lord Varuna, come and fight with me face to face. If I defeat you, you must give me passage through the ocean to take my army through to Sri Lanka.

Within minutes, the ocean became turbulent, the weather turned tempestuous and dark clouds gathered overhead. Lighting shone in streaks and thunder deafened the ears. From the depths of the ocean rose Lord Varuna in all his splendour with folded hands. "Sri Rama", he addressed Lord Rama, "I am pleased with your worship and really want to help you cross over the ocean. But contrary to the laws of Nature, I cannot part the ocean to create a path for you. But I can guarantee one boon for you. Build a *Sethu* (Ocean Bridge) across from here to Sri Lanka using rocks and wood from yonder forest. I will see that they bind together into a solid bridge from here to Sri Lanka. This *Sethu*, which you build will float in the ocean despite the large rocks that you use to construct it." With these words, Lord Varuna disappeared into the ocean.

All the monkeys and bears were overjoyed. They set about enthusiastically to build the bridge. They brought large boulders from far and wide and flung them into the sea to build the *Sethu*. There were giant monkeys and small ones. They carried stones large and small according to their ability to help build the *Sethu*. Some brought large trees from the nearby forest and used them as a lattice, in the gaps of which the others filled the stones and rocks. This went on for days without rest. The monkeys and bears were very enthusiastic when they did this and sang Lord Rama's praise as they worked day in and day out.

One day as the work was progressing, Lord Rama noticed a tiny squirrel carry a small pebble in its forepaws walk over to the *Sethu* and dump it into the crevices in the latticework. Lord Rama watched in fascination for a while as the little squirrel carried pebble after pebble and dropped it on the bridge which was slowly taking shape.

Rama watched mesmerised by the squirrel's actions. After some time, the squirrel paused, ostensibly tired, and glanced at Lord Rama. Lord Rama called out to the little creature and beckoned it to come near him. "What a noble gesture this little squirrel is doing!", said Lord Rama speaking to his brother Lakshmana who stood nearby. "Even the little squirrel wants to help in building the Rama *Sethu*. What a noble creature", he wondered. Saying so, Lord Rama stroked the back of the squirrel three times with his three fingers. The squirrel immediately regained its strength and went bounding back to do its chore of carrying pebbles to build the *Sethu*.

From that day, Indian squirrels have three white lines on their back where Lord Rama had stroked the squirrel. It is a mark of recognition that however small and insignificant you may be, you can always contribute to any mighty venture in a small way at least.

Moral: However small or insignificant you may be, do not think that you are worthless. Even minor things become important in getting big things done.

Varuna: The God of the Oceans – in Indian Mythology

Sethu: A bridge or Causeway

38. The Hermit's Ego

The kids were enjoying their vacation in India. Jaya made wry face. She was watching as the labourer was cleaning our garden. He had weeded the garden and had tilled the soil and planted a lot of saplings in my vegetable garden. He had plucked, ripe mangoes from the tree and had collected them in a basket.

Seeing Vijaya and Jaya watching him, he picked up two ripe mangoes from the basket and held them out to the kids. There was a look of surprise on their faces, but they did not accept the mangoes, but shook their heads and ran back inside.

"Why did you refuse the mangoes, kids?", I asked Jaya.

"He was all dirty and scared me. I did not feel like accepting mangoes from his dirty hands", said she wrinkling her nose.

I burst out laughing. "Ha, ha", what fools you are. All that you had to do was to accept the mangoes and wash them well before eating them. You are like the hermit who, even though he was thirsty, refused to accept water from the hunter because he was dirty."

Thathu, Thathu", they chorused in unison, and I told them the story of The Hermit's Ego…

· · · · · · · · · · · ·

Once upon a time there was a hermit who lived in a cave in the outskirts of a forest. He was very devout and spent most of his time in prayer and meditations. Every morning he used to get up before sunrise and bathe in the nearby river and then perform his prayers and daily meditation. He was always clean and tidy and never touched anything that could contaminate his austerity. Occasionally people used to visit him, and he used to give them advice on various spiritual matters. He coveted nothing and was always happy and contented. He never asked anything of anyone and used to live eating the fruits and tubers from the forest.

Once the hermit was walking along the forest when he saw a deer trapped in a snare by the side of a pond. The snare had been placed there by a hunter with a view to trap small animals. A doe was standing nearby shedding tears that it could not help its mate. Out of pity for the deer, the hermit released it from the snare and the deer along with its mate went bounding happily into the forest.

Soon, the hermit saw a divine glow emanate from the forest and a disembodied voice addressed him, "Oh, hermit, you have done well by releasing the deer from the trap. You showed true pity for the deer. I am pleased with you. Do ask any boon you would like to have. I will grant it, for I am Indra, the God of all celestial beings".

The hermit turned towards the glow and bowed. "Obeisance to thee Oh, Lord Indra", he said, "I am greatly honoured by your offer. But being an ordinary *sadhu* who has renounced everything in this world, I do not yearn for anything that gods can offer. So, I do not want anything."

"No, you must ask something", said the voice, "Once I have offered a boon to you, I cannot revoke it. Hence, you have to ask me some boon".

The hermit thought for a moment. "Oh, Lord, whenever I feel thirsty, wherever I am, I should get water to drink", he asked.

"So be it", said the voice and faded away. A moment later the light disappeared.

The hermit went on his way back to his cave for his usual meditation and penance.

Days rolled by. Once the hermit went deep into the forest and it was getting dark. The hermit felt that he was lost and was feeling very thirsty. There was no water anywhere. The hermit was at a loss as to what to do.

Suddenly, he remembered the voice of Lord Indra which had told him that he would get water to quench his thirst wherever he was. He closed his eyes and muttered a prayer.

Soon he heard barking in a distance. There appeared before him a hunter. He was holding two hunting dogs in a leash. They were tugging at the leash rearing to attack. The hunter himself was dark skinned and unclean and stinking, with a flayed carcass of a deer slung across his shoulder. His hair was matted, unkempt and brownish in colour and hung around his neck in long locks. In his left hand he held a bow and a quiver full of arrows hung from his shoulder. He held out a leather water bottle to the hermit. "Here, drink this, swami, you look very thirsty and tired".

The hermit's nose wrinkled in disgust. He could not bear the stink. He shook his head as if to say 'No'.

The hunter said again, "Swami, you are thirsty, don't you want water?"

The hermit shook his head vigorously, "No", he said, "I am not thirsty. I don't want water".

The hunter smiled sarcastically and went his way muttering something to himself.

The hermit did not look back as he could not stand the sight of the filthy specimen of humanity.

After the hunter had gone, the hermit turned his eyes towards the heavens and said, "Oh God, what did I do to be punished like this. I was promised water to quench my thirst but sending a dirty hunter like this to me with water was cruel. Why did you do it?"

Suddenly all around his there was a divine glow and the disembodied voice resonated from the forest, "Oh, hermit. I had promised to get you water whenever you were thirsty. But when I told Lord Siva about this, he offered to give you the heavenly Amruth personally instead of plain water. So, he decided to come to you himself with the Amruth in his water bottle. But you spurned him because he was in disguise as a hunter. He wanted to test you and hence he assumed the form of a hunter. You refused the divine Amruth and hence lost the golden opportunity for immortality."

The hermit was at a loss to reply.

"Your conscience was clouded by your ego which did not accept a dirty hunter as a fellow human being and hence you refused to accept water from him. You still have not learned to accept all humans as equal. You have a long way to go. However, there is water in a pond ten paces to your right. You may quench your thirst and go back to your cave." The voice faded away.

The hermit returned to his cave dejected.

Moral: Ego can mar one's path to success and achievement. All humans should be treated equally.

Indra: The King of the Devas who are the gods in heaven. He is the God of Rains and Rivers.

Sadhu: A Hindu holy man, especially one who has chosen to live apart from society

Amruth: It is the Nectar of Immortality which was obtained by churning the Milky Ocean by the Devas and Asuras according to Hindu Mythology.

Siva: One of the Trinity of Gods in Hindu mythology.

39. The Friend's Superstition

One day while they were enjoying their vacation in India with us, Jaya and Vijaya were sitting on the door sill on the veranda when our neighbour, Janaki walked in. She was an eighty-year-old widow who stayed alone in a small house near ours. Her son and daughter were working abroad, and Janaki preferred to stay alone instead of joining them abroad.

Seeing the kids sitting on the door sill at sunset, she remarked, "Children, don't sit on the door sill at sunset, it is a bad omen. You will come to harm."

The kids were taken aback as they did not understand the meaning of this superstition which the woman mentioned. They ran to my side where I was reading a book in my study. "Thathu, why is the woman saying like that? She said harm will come to us," they intoned.

"Oh, don't mind her", I said, "That is superstition. Don't bother about it". I reassured the kids, "Nothing will happen to you. There is a story about a friend who believed in superstition and got into trouble."

"Tell us that story Thathu", said the kids and I told them a story about the Friend's Superstition…

· · · · · · · · · · · ·

Once upon a time in a town, lived two friends. They were both businessmen and lived in nearby houses with their families. Their children used to play and go to school together. Their wives also were very close friends. They shared all news about their families and their woes with each other. When one family needed help the other was always there for them. They lived almost like brothers. But they had beliefs which were not alike. One of them was superstitious and believed in Astrology and the occult. Whereas the other was a more practical man who believed in the power of the mind and faced everything positively. Still, they were bosom friends.

Over a period, the superstitious friend was beset with misfortune after misfortune. Mishaps plagued him one after another. First, his son who was only fifteen years old had an accident riding his bicycle, broke his leg and was bedridden for a long time. Then his wife had a severe pain in her belly and the doctor had insisted on an emergency surgical operation to remove a lump which had grown inside her. Soon the friend himself faced losses in his business, and the banks were threatening to foreclose their mortgage and they were on the brink of losing their home. Over and above this he had a minor heart attack. All this drove him into deep depression and misery.

He approached a famous astrologer in the nearby village and was advised that there were 'evil forces' at work which were wreaking havoc on his family.

He confided all this to his friend. His friend was more pragmatic and down-to-earth and did not believe in astrology and 'evil forces'. He always believed that only hard work and a positive mindset achieved results. He advised the friend that over a period all these troubles would blow away, but the latter could not bring himself around to accept that.

Finally, the friend offered him an alternative. "I know a magician who is very good. He will be able to pinpoint your problem and get rid of the misfortune and troubles that are haunting you. I will bring him to your house to find out what is the reason for your calamities."

The friend agreed and the next day, his friend came along with the magician. The magician wore a turban, was clad in ochre clothes, and had a long staff in his hand on which was tied coloured strings of various hues. He held a *kamandal* of holy water in one hand and a string of prayer beads in the other.

His sandals were made of wood and made a peculiar 'knock' 'knock' sound while walking.

"Hari Om!", chanted the magician, "I sense that there is some spirit in this house which is causing you the trouble that you are beset with.

The friend, with folded hands entreated, "Swami, pray help me with this. How to get rid of this evil that is tormenting our family."

"I will help you", promised the magician, "Let me first find out the cause and its location."   He sat cross-legged on the floor in the centre hall of the house facing east and closed his eyes in deep meditation muttering a *mantra.*

Half an hour later he opened his eyes and said, "Bring me a brass plate with water in it. The friend's wife immediately brought a large brass plate filled with water. The magician sprinkled holy ash on the water and gazed at it for a minute and asked, "Is there a *Pala* tree in the southern corner of your compound?"

Of course, there is", said the friend. It has stood there for over ten years and is a fully grown one.

"The *Pala* tree is in full bloom now with its small white sweet-scented flowers carpeting the ground beneath. I want you to dig near the foot of the tree", the magician ordered.

Both friends along with the magician accompanying them went to the southern corner of the compound where stood a huge Pala tree with the ground surrounding it strewn with white sweet-scented flowers. The friend dug the earth on the southern side of the foot of the tree, a spot pointed out by the magician. After digging for some time, his spade struck on something. He clawed at the earth and pulled out a small idol a foot in length. The magician sprinkled some holy water on it from his *kamandal* bent down and inspected it. "Yes, this is it", he said straightening up. "This has been the source of all your troubles. It is the idol of a *kuttichathan*. This has been buried here by one of your rivals and it has been the cause of all your calamities in the past. Don't worry, I'll get rid of it, and you will have no trouble again."

The magician called for a sack and put the idol in it saying, "I will take it and bury it deep in the forest where it cannot trouble anyone anymore".

The magician collected his *Dakshina* and left the house. Everyone was happy.

The friend from then on was always cheerful and of a positive mind and never had any more troubles plaguing him. His business thrived and his debt was soon paid off.

Months later, the magician met the man who had introduced him to his friend. He asked, "Is your friend happy now? Have all his troubles gone?"

"Oh sure, he is fine and happy", the man replied. "No more troubles", he replied with a mischievous smile. "I know Swami, that you had ordered the idol of the *kuttichathan* to be buried beneath the Pala tree the previous night and 'discovered' it the next day"

The magician also smiled cunningly, "Yes, that was the only way to cure your friend of his superstitious nature and get his mind back into reality and positive thinking. Anyway, it worked. All is well that ends well."

Both went their ways smiling

Moral:	Sometimes one superstition can be cured only by another superstition. Like cures the like. A positive mind is never superstitious.

Kamandal:	An oblong water pot with a handle and a spout.
Mantra:	A word or sound repeated to aid concentration during meditation.
Pala Tree:	An 'Indian Devil Tree' is associated with demons and malicious spirits that live in them.
Kuttichathan:	An elf, a genie, or a Poltergeist.
Dakshina:	Any honorarium given to a cause, monastery, temple, spiritual guide or after a religious ritual. An honorarium to the guru for education, training, or guidance.

40. The Temple the King Built

When they had come to India on vacation, one day, Jaya was sitting in front of our Pooja Mandap after her bath with eyes closed. I was sitting nearby reading some verses from the Bhagavad Gita silently. In between, I saw Jaya smile while her eyes were closed. Vijaya who was sitting nearby could not concentrate and was picking at the straw mat on which all three of us were sitting.

After the prayers were over, I asked Jaya, "Hey dear, why were you smiling with your eyes closed? I thought you were praying".

"Yes, Thathu", she said brightly, "I was praying 'Hare Rama, Hare Krishna' silently, but I was also stringing a beautiful garland in my imagination for Sri Krishna, and I thought that when I presented the garland to him, he smiled!".

"You are bluffing!", retorted Vijaya, "You are lying to impress Thathu."

Come on kids, don't fight over this", I ended the discussion, have you heard of the story of the temples built by a King and a sage?"

"Tell us that story", pleaded the kids and I told them the story of the Temple the King built…

· · · · · · · · · · · ·

Long ago in South India there was a king with a kingdom which spanned the length and breadth of the country. He was very affluent as he had annexed many small kingdoms around his kingdom and made the kings there his serfs. They paid him regular rent in gold coins which the king spent on the welfare of his subjects.

One day the king had a strange dream. In the dream he saw a woman clad in maroon clothes instruct him to build a temple in the barren land on the eastern side of his kingdom beside the river. Before he could collect his wits, he woke up. All day he brooded over his dream and wanted to share it with someone. He called his court astrologer and told him about the dream and asked him what it meant.

"Oh king", the astrologer replied, "This is a divine command to you to build a temple for Goddess Durga at the spot specified. The woman in maroon clothes would be Goddess Durga herself. I think that we should go ahead with the project."

The king was impressed that the Goddess herself came in his dream with a request for a temple to be built for her. He immediately ordered his minister to gather the best architects in his kingdom and plan a grand temple for the goddess.

Meanwhile, in the forest nearby lived a sage in a small, thatched hut. He had been living there for a long time. He spent his time in worshipping Goddess Durga, whom he revered and prayed to everyday morning and evening. He longed to build a temple for her, but alas, being a poor sadhu, he had no money or gold to build a temple. Every night, therefore, when he went to bed, he would dream of building a temple for the goddess in his imagination. He planned a huge temple in his imagination, designed by himself. Firstly, he built the foundation of the temple. Then he carved rocks from the nearby mountain- all in his imagination. Day by day, his temple grew in his imagination whereas the real huge structure being built by the king was also coming up near the riverside.

Finally, after two long years, the king completed the temple and had to perform the main pooja – the *Kumbhabhishekam* or the consecration ceremony of the newly built temple. The beautiful idol of goddess Durga was fixed on to a pedestal in the sanctum sanctorum of the temple and all that remained was to complete the *Kumbhabhishekam* ceremony.

The king's chief astrologer fixed a day and *muhurtam* (auspicious time) on that day for the ceremony to take place. All arrangements were made and all guests from far and wide had been invited to the ceremony. It was believed that after the consecration process, the mystic power of the deity will be manifest in the idol. Till that time, the idol is but a statue carved in granite.

That night the king had a strange dream. The same goddess clad in maroon clothes appeared in his dream and said, "Oh, king. I am impressed with the temple that you have built for me. It is huge and the architecture is eye-catching. But for tomorrow's *Kumbhabhishekam*, I will not be able to come to your temple as I will be partaking in another *Kumbhabhishekam* in another part of your kingdom for an equally huge temple."

The king was surprised and at the same time annoyed. He asked the woman in his dream. "Oh, mother, who has built another temple in my kingdom without my knowledge. I must see him."

The goddess smiled and said, "Far away in the forest lives a sage who has been building a temple in his imagination for the past two years and he too is consecrating his imaginary temple on the same day at the same *muhurtam* as you. I will be attending that ceremony, not yours."

"But Oh, Goddess Durga", the king asked, "Why are you so keen to attend the ceremony and pooja of an 'imaginary' temple and not my real temple? What made you want to do that?"

The goddess smiled, "My dear king, you have built your temple with mere brick and mortar. But my devotee, the sage has done so with real love, devotion, and sincerity. His devotion is a thousand times more than yours".

The goddess disappeared. The king woke up and immediately, summoned his minister and astrologer and explained his dream to them. The astrologer advised him to go to the forest and meet the pious sage whom the goddess had favoured over him.

The next morning, the king along with the minister and the astrologer went to the forest in search of the sage and found him meditating beneath a banyan tree near his hut. The king prostrated before him saying, "Oh *Mahatma*, your devotion is a thousand times greater than mine as the goddess came in my dream and said that she will be attending your *Kumbhabhishekam* and not mine which I had planned for today. So, you must accompany me to my palace and help me in the *Kumbhabhishekam* of my temple."

The sage looked bewildered for a moment and then smiled. He said, "In a way, oh mighty king, you are superior to me, and your devotion is greater than mine. Goddess Durga chose to come in your dream twice and command you to build a temple for her. But despite my years of penance and prayers, not once did she appear before me or in my dream. In that way, you are more blessed than I am. I built a temple in my imagination only, but She made you build a temple and made each of us meet the other to culminate in the *Kumbhabhishekam*. I will gladly accompany you to your palace to conduct the ceremonies."

The sage and the king with his retinue, came back to the palace and conducted the Kumbhabhishekam to the satisfaction of everyone.

The sage refused to accept any *dakshina* from the king saying that what he did was a labour of love and devotion and could not be measured in gold or silver. He went back to his frugal living in the hut in the forest and the king continued his good work.

Moral:	Devotion to God is not just in spending wealth for various activities, it is real love of God in one's mind that matters.

Kumbhabhishekam:	It is a consecration ceremony to homogenize, synergize and unite the mystic powers of the deity in a newly built temple.
Muhurtam:	Auspicious time. One muhurtam is 48 minutes.
Mahatma:	A revered person regarded with love and respect; a holy person or sage
Dakshina:	Any honorarium given to a cause, monastery, temple, spiritual guide or after a religious ritual. An honorarium to the guru for education, training, or guidance.

About the Author

Dr. K. V. Sahasranam is a practicing Senior Consultant Cardiologist and Former Chief of Medical Services in a Multispecialty hospital in Calicut, Kerala. He holds an M.D. degree in General Medicine and a Doctorate in Cardiology. He has a professional experience of over 45 years and is the author of more than forty scientific papers in National and International Journals.

This book is his second venture at publication of a book. His first book was titled, "Tell Me a Story, Grandpa." Written under the name 'Sahasranam Kalpathy', this book is a collection of short stories which he has gathered over years from his parents, grandparents and various other sources like magazines, Indian Mythology, religious discourses, and from friends and teachers. He has ventured to compile them into an anthology of short stories for his grandchildren and children of ages 9 to 12. He has been greatly influenced writing these stories from the Moral Science classes of his teachers in St Joseph's Boys High School in Calicut where he studied.

This book is the second in the series of Short Stories for Children

He is happily married and lives with his wife in Calicut in Kerala, India. His two daughters are well settled and live in the United States of America.

He is contemplating writing a Part 3 for this anthology of short stories.

Contact him and give your honest feedback:

Email: kvsauthor@gmail.com

URL: https://www.amazon.com/author/sahasranamkalpathy

Medium: https://medium.com/me/stories/public

Medium: https://medium.com/subscribe/@ramani2911

Linked In: https://www.linkedin.com/in/sahasranam-dr-k-v-3231a13a/

137

Made in the USA
Columbia, SC
03 December 2022

72656490R00076